CW01021381

ESCORTING MISS MERCER

A SAPPHIC AGE GAP ROMANCE IN THE 1940S

AVEN BLAIR

Copyright Page

© 2024 Aven Blair. All rights reserved.
No part of this book may be reproduced, distributed, or transmitted in any
form or by any means, including photocopying, recording, or other
electronic or mechanical methods, without the prior written permission of
the publisher, except in the case of brief quotations embodied in critical
reviews and certain other noncommercial uses permitted by copyright law.

ALSO BY AVEN BLAIR

Claire's Young Flame

Julian's Lady Luck

Evan's Entanglement

My Sapphires only Dance for Her

Driving Miss Kennedy

Sailing Miss Clarkson

Flying Miss Lomax

CHAPTER ONE: EMERY

Savannah, Georgia
January 1948

As I climb the stairs from my antique warehouse to my loft apartment, I have only one thing on my mind: taking a very long, warm bath. Most of my day was spent restoring a Wardrobe that *The Wilde House,* my antique business, purchased a few days ago. The scent of aged wood and polish still lingers on my hands, a reminder of the hours I devoted to bringing the piece back to life.

After cleaning and restoring the Waring & Gillow wardrobe, I now reek of the mineral spirits I used to remove the polish from my hands. As I undress, I turn on the warm water and let the tub fill.

As I'm about to step into the warm water, my phone rings. "Damn!" I shout.

"Hello," I say a bit tartly.

"Did I catch you at a bad time, Em? You sound upset."

"No, Mom. Sorry, I was just about to take a bath. What's up?"

"Well, honey, a couple I showed a house to on Jones Street wants to view it again this evening, and they're serious buyers. I'm supposed to pick Ingrid up at the airport, but now I'm stuck. They're too important to cancel or reschedule."

"Honey, could you please pick Ingrid up from the airport? I want her to be greeted by someone other than a taxi. She's family, and she needs…"

"Okay, Mom, I can do that. What time is her flight?"

"It's scheduled to arrive at 7:15."

"Mom, you do realize it's already 6:00, don't you?"

"Yes, Em. Can you take a quick bath and still make it, honey?"

"Yes, Mom, it's no problem. I'll do it."

"Thank you, Em. Oh, by the way, could you swing by and pick up the Packard? I know you love your Willys Jeep, but you can't pick Ingrid up in *'that thing.'*"

"So, I'm supposed to bathe and dress, then swing by your house to pick up a proper car, and then meet her in an hour and fifteen minutes."

"Oh, honey, you can do it."

"No problem, Mom. Let me go so I can take a quick bath."

Sinking in the tub, I'm not sure if I'm irritated at Mom or just nervous about seeing Ingrid. I think to myself: *'You'd better pull yourself together before you pick up the woman you've had a crush on since you were sixteen.'*

As I plunge under the water, I linger momentarily, revisiting a memory from twelve years ago when I gave Ingrid a short love note.

Over the years, whenever she returned home to Savannah, she always greeted me with genuine kindness and affection. Even after my awkward attempt to give her that

2

intimate note at her Oscar party here in Savannah, her warmth never wavered, only deepening my feelings for her.

Emerging from the water, I chuckle to myself, thinking, "What a silly girl I was." I can't help but wonder why on earth I ever thought Ingrid Mercer would want to be my girlfriend, lover, or anything else. I continue laughing as I bathe in record time.

Rummaging through my closet, I glance at my watch and see that it's 6:25. I don't have a clue what to wear. Grabbing a pair of black Chinos and a Gray Cardigan, I toss them on the bed and return to the bathroom mirror. "Grrrr, thanks, Mom!" I have fifty minutes to dry my hair, get dressed, pick up the Packard, and dash to the airport.

Expelling a massive breath, I look at myself and say, "That's too much. What can I mark off?" I'll definitely need to towel dry my wet hair. Grabbing my towel, I start drying my thick, short mane. Squeezing my hair with the towel, I laugh at myself, finally realizing why I'm so upset.

Removing the towel, I stand in front of the bathroom mirror, completely nude, and run my hands through my hair. Gazing at my reflection I say, "You're still crazy about Ingrid."

Picking up the brush, I run it through my hair, shake it loose, and style it with my fingers, pushing it back and to the left. Then, I toss the brush in the sink.

After putting on my chinos and cardigan, I slip into my favorite pair of loafers, sit on the chair in my bedroom, and glance at my watch. It's 6:45. Why has it taken me forty-five minutes to make such little progress? I bury my face in my hands and rest my elbows on my knees. I'm aware that I still have unresolved feelings for Ingrid, but that was so long ago. I spray a bit of cologne on myself just before dashing down the steps of my antique warehouse building.

As I jump into my Willys Jeep, I say out loud, "Sorry, Mom, but Ingrid's going to have to ride in '*this thing*' tonight."

I crank her up, shift into first gear, and roll onto Abercorn Street toward the airport.

As I drive, I thread my fingers through my hair, trying to dry it with the wind. It's cold as hell. I should have brought a blanket for Ingrid.

Approaching the airport entrance, I feel nervous. I pull over briefly to fuss with my hair. Thank goodness I have great hair, like everyone tells me, or I would never be able to pull off my hair drying like this.

Pulling the rearview mirror toward me, I look at myself and push my fingers back through my hair one last time before approaching the front entrance. Scanning the area, I don't see Ingrid outside or through the vast windows. Glancing at my watch, I see it's 7:25.

Finally, I catch a glimpse of her walking gracefully through the terminal, with a Porter carrying her baggage. She's still as gorgeous as she was twelve years ago.This should be interesting when she sees me instead of Mom and the Jeep instead of a more appropriate vehicle like the Packard.

Jumping out of the Jeep, I greet her as she exits the building.

"Emery!" She shouts, running toward me. My gosh, you've grown up; look at you!" Ingrid grabs me in a bear hug, just like she always did. Her Southern accent and that warm embrace are two things she chose to keep. I love them both, but the bear hug is especially welcome right now.

Wanting her to see how much I've grown up, I draw her close and give her a confident, warm hug. She mutters, "Hmmm," then begins to release me.

"Hi, Ingrid," I say softly. Determined to be the one to end the hug, I hold her a bit longer, before kissing her cheek as I release her.

"Well, my goodness, Emery Wilde, you've developed some

confident charisma and charm over the years. I mean, you always had it, but now—hmmm." She says as she gazes into my eyes. All I can do is grin.

"You might not find me too charming when you see what I'm picking you up in. And you can thank Mom for that."

As we walk toward my Willys Jeep, Ingrid starts laughing out loud. "This has to be your vehicle, Emery. Hell, honey, I don't give a damn what you pick me up in. Besides, I'd rather you pick me up than Lillian. She's my best friend, but you and I need to catch up."

The porter looks at me oddly as I ask him to put the luggage in the back of the Willys. Ingrid doesn't miss a beat; she jumps into the passenger's seat and laughs again.

"What a great surprise! I get tired of limousines and drivers. This is a treat, baby," she says with heightened enthusiasm.

"Well, Mom will kill me tomorrow. I was supposed to go to her house and get the Packard, but I didn't have time. I'm sorry."

"Don't be sorry, Emery. Let's go, girl. Drive me to the Savannah Hilton and pull right up front. Let's give them something to talk about."

Ingrid's southern charm is still intact and is working on me as I crank the Willys and head toward the Hotel. "How fast will this thing go, Emery?"

Grinning at her, I say, "Well, Willys wasn't made for speed, but we can try her out if you like."

"Yes! Let's go. If you get a ticket, I'll take care of it."

Doing my best to please and impress this Hollywood vixen, my teenage crush, I press the pedal firmly. The engine roars to life, and soon, we're cruising up Montgomery Street at sixty miles per hour. Ingrid laughs, pulling her fur coat tighter around her neck.

"Is this too fast? You look cold."

"I'm freezing, but this is exhilarating. Can you go a little faster, Emery?"

Nervously, I press the gas pedal further, and we accelerate rapidly. Ingrid laughs, her gaze fixed on me. I'm starting to worry that Ingrid might be trouble. From what I've gathered from Mom and the tabloids, Ingrid's always been a bit reckless, and it seems she hasn't changed with age. And she has aged quite nicely.

"Okay, Emery. You can slow her down now. I don't want to have to explain to Lillian why her youngest daughter is in jail." Thank goodness. I was about to give up on impressing her for the sake of safety.

"I'm sorry, sweetie. I am just so glad to be home again. I've missed Savannah so much." She shouts with laughter. "Can you drive Willys on the beach?"

Grinning, I glance at Ingrid and say, "She's been on the beach many times."

"Good! Then you have to promise me a date on the beach with her," she says, grinning and giving me a wink.

I take a deep breath, hold it, and then exhale slowly, trying to calm my nerves. "Okay, I promise you a date at the beach."

She leans toward me and says, "And I mean at night."

I glance at her twice, trying to read her face. *'At Night'?* What does that mean? Shaking my head, I pull up to the front entrance of the Savannah Hilton.

CHAPTER TWO: INGRID

E mery charmed me with a thrilling ride from the airport to the Hotel. After checking into my suite with the help of a bellhop and Emery, I'm ready to relax for the evening. "Have a seat, Emery."

Glancing at Emery, I smile. She's grown up over the years and is utterly gorgeous. As I fuss with my luggage, I can't help but steal glances at her while she sits patiently on the sofa.

"I'm going to order us a bottle of Champagne, Emery. Will you stay a while so we can catch up?"

She looks at me a bit apprehensively. As I wait for her reply, I gaze into her beautiful gray eyes.

"Well, I don't know, Ingrid. Maybe I should get back to the warehouse.

"Do you have other plans?"

"No, I just thought maybe you've had a long day and could use some rest."

Sitting on the other end of the sofa from her, I say, "It has been a long day. It took me twelve hours to get here, so now I want to celebrate. I want to celebrate with you, Emery."

She grins at me and says, "Sure, I'll stay a while. And no, I don't have any other plans."

"Great!" I say enthusiastically as I get up to call room service. "I'll order the champagne now and then arrange for some food later."

After the champagne arrives, I pour a glass for each of us and gaze at Emery. "What should we toast to?" I ask her.

"Let me think," she says, looking away momentarily.

"Well, all I can think of is making a toast to you being back home in Savannah."

"Okay, then let's toast to Savannah." We clink our glasses together and share a chuckle, smiling at each other.

"This is good champagne, Ingrid. I'm glad you asked me to stay."

"Thank you for accepting. It makes me happy to share my first evening home with you," I say sincerely.

"What have you been up to lately, Emery?"

Emery sips her champagne, gazing at me with her haunting gray eyes. "Mostly just work. For the past eight years, I've lived and breathed *The Wilde House*. I suppose I'm a bit obsessed with it."

"Emery, that's understandable. Such dedication is what makes someone successful, dear. I'm very proud of you. I always knew you'd make your mark in Savannah, and it seems I was right. From what your Mama tells me, *The Wilde House* is a huge success."

Emery grins at me and takes another sip of champagne, her body language suggesting she's a bit uneasy about my praise. "Well, Mama has a way of making things seem grander than they really are. You know that."

"Perhaps she can, but I doubt that's the case here. Emery, honey, you started this business when you were only twenty. Who does that? I can assure you, I don't know any other young women who have. Stop being so modest, honey."

Emery smiles at me. I hold my glass out and say, "A toast to *The Wilde House*!" She clinks her glass with mine and then gives me a charming grin, her chilling eyes locked on mine.

Sipping my champagne, I watch Emery as she talks about her business. I can't help but be incredibly drawn to her. Her facial structure and prominent cheekbones are strikingly handsome. Her thick honey-colored hair is short and tousled, swept to one side with a few strands falling over her forehead. She's truly beautiful.

"Tell me what movie you're working on now, Ingrid?" Feeling a bit uneasy and tipsy from the champagne, I rest my arm on the back of the sofa and take another sip.

"Emery, when you reach my age, the parts are fewer, honey, and they start to completely dry up," I say, my tone growing somber as I reflect on my career. The room falls quiet.

Emery extends her arm on the sofa, her hand touches mine. Instinctively, I interlace my fingers with hers. Though I know this might not be wise, I choose to ignore it as Emery accepts my touch and gazes at me tenderly.

"Ingrid, you're still a gorgeous woman. You must have many roles available to you. Gazing at our interlaced fingers, I tenderly rub her thumb with mine.

Looking at her, I say, "Emery, most of the leading roles go to women your age, honey. Once you hit forty, the leading roles are pretty much over. I get offers for parts like *'The Mother'* or other supporting roles. There's nothing wrong with those, but when you've spent your career as a leading lady, accepting them can feel like a bit of a kick in the stomach."

"I'm sorry, Ingrid. I can see how that would make you feel," she says, rubbing her thumb against mine as our fingers remain interlaced.

"Oh, Emery. It's okay, sweetie. I've known this day would

come for years. Now that it's here, I just need to decide what I want my life to look like over the next twenty years or more."

"What do you mean, Ingrid?"

"I mean, am I going to remain in Hollywood or return to Savannah while I'm still on top?'

"You think you'd be happy back in Savannah?"

"I have no idea, but I'm at a crossroads and I need to decide." Looking at Emery, I feel her genuine concern for me, and it warms my heart. I think of the love note she gave me when she was sixteen, and I smile.

"Savannah would welcome you back with open arms for you if you chose to come home, Ingrid. That would be amazing, but only if it would make you happy."

"How did you get so wise, Emery Wilde?"

Laughing, she says, "I don't feel very wise, Ingrid, but I appreciate that you think so."

Reluctantly removing my fingers from hers, I lean close to her and whisper, "More champagne or food?"

Emery, obviously feeling the effects of the bottle we just finished, leans towards me and whispers, "How about both." Then she exclaims, "Oh damn! I forgot to move my Willys from the front entrance. I better go move it now."

As she stands, I say, "Give me your keys, Emery."

She hands them to me and asks, "You're not going to move it, are you?"

Choking on my last sip of champagne, I start laughing and giggling at her. As I continue to giggle and cough, I hug her, taking in her intoxicating blend of citrus and musk.

"No! You crazy woman! I'm calling the front desk to ask them to move it. You sit back down." Emery and I both start giggling as I walk to the phone.

As I pick up the receiver, Emery shouts, "Tell them to treat her with kindness."

Breaking into laughter, I put the receiver down and say, "Hush, Emery! Don't get me tickled again."

Walking back to the couch, I say, "I forgot how funny you are, Emery."

"Well, I was a bit puzzled about how you were going to crawl up in *'that thing,'* as Mama calls it, and re-park it." We both roar with laughter.

After we finish laughing, Emery and I continue talking about our lives while we wait for room service.

"Tell me about your love life, Emery. Anyone serious?"

"You have to tell me about yours first, Ingrid," she says boldly.

"No, I don't. I asked you first. Go ahead and spill it. Tell me all about her."

"Her?" I ask, giving her a quizzical look.

"Emery! You can't sit here and tell me someone as wonderful and uniquely charming as you is dating men. I'd be thoroughly disappointed."

"Disappointed? Why?"

"You know damn well why, Emery Wilde."

Gazing at me mischievously, she says, "Yeah, I guess you know I have no interest in men, don't you?"

I nod, "You're safe with me, love."

"Really? You never told Mom about the note I gave you a hundred years ago?"

Giving her a blank stare, I say, "Emery, you can't possibly think I told Lillian about that note." Moving closer to her, I thread my fingers through her thick hair and add, "I've never told anyone. That sweet love note has remained between us."

"Thank you, Ingrid. Many times, I've been embarrassed that I gave it to you."

Reaching for my clutch, I silently remove my wallet finding the note hidden in the back. Pulling it out gently, I look at Emery and say, "You clearly have no idea what this note means to me."

Her eyes grow wide as she looks at it. "That's it, Ingrid? You still have my note?"

"Why wouldn't I, Emery? Honey, I've always been very fond of you, and this note has brought me a lot of comfort over the years.Whenever I'd get down or needed to feel some love from home, I'd pull your tender note out and read it."

Emery runs her fingers through her hair and leans her arm against the top of the sofa. With her fingers still in her locks of hair, she looks at me and smiles sweetly.

"That makes me feel extremely important to you, knowing you've kept my note, Ingrid."

"Honey, you're very important to me."

We hear a knock on the door. "That must be room service. Will you let them in, Emery, while I put my note away?"

"I sure will." She walks swiftly toward the door. As her back is turned to me, I kiss her note and tuck it safely back to where it's remained for years.

CHAPTER THREE: EMERY

Opening the door for the bellhop, I feel slightly tipsy from the champagne. I only remember eating breakfast, so that's most likely why it hit me like this.

After he leaves the food in front of the sofa, I look at Ingrid and say, "I'd better eat something; I'm feeling a bit lightheaded."

"Emery, grab some bread quickly and eat it. I'll be right back." While I wait, I break off a piece of French bread and begin to chew, closing my eyes and taking deep breaths with each bite. I feel Ingrid sit beside me, and her exotic fragrance fills the air, intensifying my lightheadedness. She smells incredible.

"Here, Emery. Let me place this on your neck. Lean back, sweetie." As I lean against the back of the sofa, Ingrid places a cold cloth against my neck. "That helps, Ingrid. Thank you," I say with my eyes still closed. She stays beside me, turning the cool cloth over every few seconds. Is her being this close actually helping? I find myself completely powerless.

Opening my eyes, I gaze at her. "When did you last eat, Emery?"

"Ummm, this morning," I say softly.

"This morning?! This is my fault for giving you champagne on an empty stomach," she says as she continues fussing over me. "Here, love, eat some more bread." Ingrid moves her hands to my hair and threads her fingers through it. She has no idea what effect this is having on me.

"You have the most amazing hair, Emery. I think I could play in it for hours."

Feeling better, I look at her seriously and say, "That might not be a good idea, Ingrid."

Grinning at me, she flirtatiously says, "Why not? You're old enough now." Then she winks at me and laughs. Oh, heaven help me. Why is she flirting with me like this?

"You look better. How do you feel?"

"Much better, thank you. The bread and cool cloth helped."

"Good, let's eat then. Okay?" she says as she smiles and slowly removes her hand from my hair.

As we eat, we discuss her plans for this visit to Savannah. "Ingrid, Mom tells me you've come home to settle the estate and the house. Is that right?"

"Yes, that's the main reason. The house has been vacant for the four years since Mama's death. I've had someone check on it and clean it every week, but I need to decide what to do with it. My decision about the house coincides with my need to make a choice about my career. Or perhaps fate has stepped in."

"It's on Whitemarsh Island, isn't it?"

"Yes, it's right on the water. It's an ideal place to live. If I decide to keep it and live there, I would want to renovate it.

"I remember going there a couple of times when I was young. Your mom was always very kind to me, Ingrid. Each

14

time before we left, she would give me a silver dollar. You don't forget that kind of kindness as an adult."

Ingrid smiles at me and chuckles, "Yes, Mama loved giving silver dollars to you and other kids who might drop in. You're right; she was a kind soul."

"You could turn that place into a dream, Ingrid. The location is ideal; you could make it a real showplace."

Ingrid crosses her legs, picks up her champagne glass, and gazes at me. "I could with your help," she says smoothly, then takes a sip of champagne, keeping her eyes on me.

I chuckle, "My help? Ingrid, I'm not a decorator; I own an antique shop. I do, however, have a lot of amazing pieces in my warehouse that would look great in the home."

"Well, that's what I meant, but I know you have a good eye, Emery. Will you go over there with me tomorrow?"

My heart flips backward, and my extremities tingle with sensual excitement. With my heart racing, I asked, "Why me instead of Mom?"

"Because I like being with you, Emery. And I thought you could give me a tour of *The Wilde House.*" She watches me for my reaction and then grins because she sees the answer on my face. She then says, "And…"

Grinning, I ask, "And?"

She whispers, "I thought you could take me out in Willys on the beach tomorrow night."

I quickly think about my plans for tomorrow. Nothing is pressing, and it isn't every day that Ingrid Mercer asks you to spend the day with her. So you better say yes, like you want to. Don't be a fool.

Lifting my champagne glass to her, I grin and say, "You got a date, Miss Mercer."

She screams with excitement, then hugs me tightly, her fingers gently running through my hair. Damn, she feels good against me, and the way she runs her fingers through my hair is utterly seductive yet calming.

As the night goes on, we continue talking about my antique warehouse, Mom, and their friendship. "It's gotten late, Emery, and by the way, you aren't going anywhere."

"I can't stay here, Ingrid. I should get back to the loft in my warehouse."

"I've already hidden your keys, love. So you might as well get comfortable. I'll find you something to sleep in."

"Ingrid, I'm fine to drive. Just let me have my keys, please."

She digs through her large suitcase and says, "Here's a long-sleeved sleep shirt for you. It will be big on you, but it should be comfy."

"And where am I supposed to sleep?"

"With me, silly."

"Ingrid, that would be inappropriate," I say, panic rising in my voice.

She walks over to me and asks, "Who's going to know?" *Oh hell, what have I gotten myself into?* "Or you can sleep on the couch if you prefer. I just know you shouldn't drive after drinking and getting lightheaded."

"You're right, Ingrid. But I better sleep on the couch," I say, watching her for a reaction. The bed would be much more comfortable, and I'm not going to lie—that's exactly where I want to sleep. I take the sleep shirt from her and look at the bed. "Well, I'll admit the bed does look more comfortable than this sofa."

"Good! It's big enough for us. It looks king-sized, so we'll both have plenty of room." I change into the long-sleeve sleep shirt but leave my chinos on, then kick off my black loafers.

"Eyeing the oversized sleep shirt that's practically drowning me, I glance over at Ingrid with a chuckle. 'So, tell me, whose sleep shirt is this?'"

Giggling, she says, "I don't kiss and tell, Emery."

"Well, it's obviously a man's sleep top. Was it one of your leading men?" I ask, laughing.

"Yes, it was. I can tell you that much."

"Seriously, oh my gosh, I can't believe this. What else do you have in that luggage?" I ask, walking over to it and pretending to rummage through it."

"You can look through it, Emery. I don't care."

"I'm Just teasing you. But are you carrying other items that belong to your leading men?"

As she pulls her nightwear out, she lifts her eyes to meet mine and coolly says, "No, but sometimes I carry items that belong to my leading ladies."

I gaze at her in disbelief and ask slowly, "Your leading ladies?"

Offering me her hand, I take it, and our fingers intertwine. She leads me back to the sofa, and we sit. "Are you surprised, Emery?"

I look at her for a moment searching her face, "Yes, I suppose I am. Maybe the real question is, should I be?"

"That's very perceptive of you, Emery. And no, you shouldn't be surprised. If you think about it for a while, you'll realize that you shouldn't be surprised at all."

As I lean back against the sofa, I am amazed that Ingrid Mercer just basically confessed to me that she sleeps with women. I try to think about her question: *'Am I surprised?'*

"Maybe I'm not surprised, Ingrid. But I am surprised that you shared it with me."

"Why, Emery. I know that you're a sapphic. Your honesty is quite refreshing, and I trust you, love." My head is spinning. Wow. My teenage crush, whom I've fantasized about for so long, has just confessed her love of women to me in the coziness of her hotel suite.

She leans against the sofa close to me and says, "It's nice having someone who understands. It's nice talking to *you,*

17

Emery. I mean, you're grown now, so I don't want to keep it from you anymore."

"Thank you, Ingrid. You obviously know you're safe with me, with what you tell me," I say as I reach for her hands. Our fingers interlace, and she looks at them, then back at me, and smiles. "Are you okay?" I ask.

"Yes, Emery. I just feel a bit vulnerable all of a sudden." I move closer, wrap my arms around her, and pull her in.

"It must be very hard to keep a secret like this." Holding her close, I inhale her scent and feel her warmth. Though the hug was to comfort her, her allure is overwhelming. Pulling away slowly, I look at her and smile.

"Emery Wilde, you're so damn adorable with your perfect jaw and hair," she says, threading her fingers through a few strands of my hair. "Are you feeling sleepy, sweetie?"

"I don't know. What time is it?" I ask, glancing at my watch. "Wow, it's 1 a.m." We both laugh.

Touching my face, she says, "Let's get you to bed. I'm sure you have lots to do in the morning before I steal you away for the rest of the day and evening." Grinning at her, I shake my head as we share the stillness of the night for a few more moments.

"I've never actually regretted giving you that note, Ingrid."

Cupping my cheek, she says, "I hope not, Emery. I would hate to think that I carried such a sweet part of you all these years in vain."

"You haven't, Ingrid," I whisper.

"Good!" She says, then winks at me. "Are you ready for bed?"

"Yes, I'm sleepy and need to be back at the warehouse early."

"What time do you need to get up? I'll call the front desk and ask them for a wake-up call."

"I'm thinking, six… no, make it seven." She smiles at me. I

remove my pants, crawl into the bed, and roll on my side, continuing to watch Ingrid.

I'll be back in a minute," she says, then enters the bathroom and closes the door. I put my hands to my face, grinning the biggest grin I can ever remember having. I'll be sharing a bed with Ingrid Mercer, my long-time crush, tonight. And I've just learned that she sleeps with women. I'm overwhelmed with a million sensations running through my body and mind.

Closing my eyes, I picture her beautiful face—her laughter as I drove my Willys, and her fingers brushing through my hair. When I open my eyes, I see her standing at the bedside. She smiles at me, then picks up the phone receiver. "Yes, please ring my room for a wake-up call at seven a.m.," she says, winking at me. "Thank you." She then places the receiver back on the cradle.

"I'm exhausted, love, so don't worry about me trying to get fresh with you." She glances at me, giggles, then crawls into bed and turns towards me.

"Oh, Ingrid, why would I think that?"

"Obviously, you don't realize what a catch you are, Miss Wilde." She says with a grin, then yawns and rolls over. "Good night, love, I had a wonderful evening with you."

"Goodnight, Ingrid. Thank you. I had a great time with you." As I lay in the muted darkness, I gaze at her silhouette and dark curls. I begin to think of the many things she told me tonight, especially her last comment: *"Obviously you don't realize what a catch you are, Miss Wilde."*

If we weren't so exhausted, I would crawl up next to her, pull her against me, and inhale her intoxicating scent all night. I can't even imagine how wonderful she would feel in my arms and against my breast. Closing my eyes, I feel myself drifting off peacefully.

CHAPTER FOUR: INGRID

T he phone jolts me awake at seven a.m. I hear Emery gets out of bed and answer the call with a quick "Thank you" before hanging up. Soft morning light bathes the room through the large windows.

I'm still half asleep but can't help watching as Emery removes her nightshirt. A glimpse of her lovely, perfect breast stirs something sensual within me. She's just as I imagined, unaware that I'm watching her undress. After putting on her black brassiere, she quickly pulls her gray cardigan over her head, giving me a full view of her long, toned legs and stomach.

She glances over at me and freezes. "I didn't know you were watching me."

"Why shouldn't I? You're a beauty, Emery Wilde."

"And, you're trouble, Ingrid Mercer."

Laughing, I say, "Don't believe everything you hear or read about me, love."

Emery continues to dress in front of me, then walks back to the bed and sits beside me. "I had a great time last night. What time do you want to get together today?"

"Well, I'll call your Mama in a bit and invite her for breakfast or coffee. You let me know what time works for you."

"How about twelve or one o'clock? Is that okay?"

As I play with a few strands of her hair, I say, "Sure, love. Pick me up in the Willys at one o'clock, and we can head to the house. Will that be good?"

"That sounds great; I'll see you then."

"Hold on one minute, ma'am. You'd better hug me good-bye. Don't get all weird after my confession last night."

Emery looks at me seriously and says, "I would never do that, Ingrid. Thank you for opening up to me." She gives me a strong hug, looks into my eyes, and kisses my cheek. "Bye, I'll see you at one o'clock. Oh, and I found my keys, by the way. Don't you know the freezer is the first place crooks and perverse people always look?"

Grinning, I look at her and say, "Perverse, huh?" She swipes her fingers through her sexy hair, smiles, and waves goodbye as she leaves.

Pulling the covers over my head, I fall sideways on the bed, wondering what that charming twenty-eight-year-old woman has done to me. She's made me act like a damn forty-six-year-old fool, for one thing.

Uncovering myself, I grab her pillow and push mine away. I lie on her pillow and inhale her scent. My feminine region pulses as I smell her and think of last evening with her. Why did I admit my love for women to her? Was it only because I knew she would understand?

Emery opened her heart to me twelve years ago. She's a grown woman, so it felt cathartic and appropriate to bear my heart to her last night. Was that the reason, or is it because she is now old enough for me to *"find her,"* as she stated in her romantic love note she gave me moons ago?

I rise, retrieve the note, and crawl back into bed with it.

Slowly, I open it to read it for the millionth time. It simply reads:

Dear Ingrid,
A fleeting glance, a moment's touch,
In every silent beat, I feel your presence.
When the world aligns, and your heart is free,
Find me, for though I am young, I'll wait for you patiently.
Yours always,
Emery

I realize that sixteen-year-old Emery wrote that to thirty-four-year-old Ingrid. Yet, the love note feels remarkably new and fresh, as if it was written while I slept and slipped under my pillow just before I woke.

Walking into *Old Towne Café*, I spot Lillian at a back corner table. She sees me and stands to greet me. "Ingrid!" she calls out as I run to her. Memories from years ago flash back, and I think of how she let me join her group of older girls. She would always say, "'I simply adore you, kid.'"

"I never feel like I'm home until I get my official Lillian hug," I tell her sincerely.

"Ingrid, you feel so good. And you're still drop-dead gorgeous, honey. It's been way too long," she says as we release one another. "I've ordered you coffee."

"Good, and thank you. Lillian, you look amazing. I see where Emery gets her looks from. Honey, that girl is flawless!"

"She's an original, I'll say that, and I wouldn't change a thing about her," Lillian says as she sips her coffee. "She and Anne are complete opposites. How does that happen?"

"I don't know, but I'll tell you this. Anne might be a beauty and a real Southern Belle, but honey, she ain't got the charm and charisma that Emery has. And I admit that Anne is beautiful, but Emery is handsomely gorgeous. If I took her to Hollywood, I could have that girl in movies within a week."

Lillian laughs, leans into me, and says, "Well, you know parents aren't supposed to have favorites, and if you tell anyone I said this, I'll cut your tongue out." Then she sips her coffee and looks at me.

"Say what, Lillian?"

She leans closer and says, "I have four children, Ingrid, but I've always had a special closeness with Emery that I've never found with the others. She just has a different kind of soul."

Nodding, I say, "That's exactly what she has, Lillian. I couldn't have said it more perfectly."

"She told me about the airport pickup. I would apologize for not picking you up in a more proper car, but she said you enjoyed the ride."

"It was exhilarating! Like I told her, I get tired of limousines and drivers. I felt like a real Savannahian when we flew down Montgomery Street last night. I haven't laughed that much in years."

"Well, I'm glad you enjoyed yourself. Em says she's taking you to the house today. I would love to join you, but my afternoon is booked with clients. Please let me know next time you decide to come home so I can cross off days for us. I miss you, Ingrid."

"I know, Lillian, and I miss you too. It was just a spur-of-the-moment decision. January is quiet for me; I don't have anything shooting this month, so I thought, 'Hell, I'll go home to Savannah and surround myself with people who love and know the real Ingrid.'"

"How long are you here for?"

"I haven't decided, to be honest. I might stay all month. I need to figure out what to do with the house."

"You're not thinking of selling it, are you?"

"Oh, Lillian, I don't know. I told Emery last night, and might as well tell you—I've been thinking about moving home."

Lillian's mouth flies open, and she stares at me in disbelief. "Seriously?"

"Yep," I say and sip my coffee.

"Ingrid Mercer is thinking of giving up Hollywood for Savannah, Georgia." Lillian places her hand on my forehead and says, "Honey, let me check you for a fever; you're obviously sick."

"I'm dead serious, Lillian."

"Well, honey, that's incredible, but what on earth will you do here? I know you don't have to work anymore, but you still need to stay busy."

"I'll figure it out as I go along, Lillian."

"Okay, Friday night dinner at my house. Honey, we are celebrating; this is joyful!"

"That would be great. I'd love to have dinner at your house. It's a date!"

"Good. Why don't you stay with Ted and me instead of the hotel."

"Lillian, we go through this every time I visit. You know I prefer staying at a hotel and then visiting everyone. It's simply more enjoyable for me."

"I understand. You've always preferred this, but I must try to get you to sleep over like in the old days."

Laughing, I say, "Lillian, we ain't thirteen and seventeen

anymore. Why on earth did you let a silly thirteen-year-old become one of the cool kids at school?"

"Hell, you know the answer to that, Ingrid," she says with a laugh. Then, taking my cheeks in her hands, she adds, "I simply adore you, kid.'"

"Lillian, you always made me feel so special. I love you, honey."

"And I love you, Ingrid. You're incredibly special. You always have been."

CHAPTER FIVE: EMERY

Driving back to the Savannah Hilton to pick up Ingrid, I feel excited and almost giddy—a sensation that's unfamiliar and a bit uncomfortable. Pulling off the road like last night, I sit and take deep breaths to calm myself. Glancing in the rearview I think about Ingrid's last words before we went to sleep: *"Obviously, you don't realize what a catch you are, Miss Wilde."*

Fussing with my hair for a minute I then nod and chuckle before steering Willys back onto the road toward the hotel. Pulling up to the front entrance I park a little away from the entrance, mindful that they might associate *"this thing"* with Miss Mercer. I don't want to appear too audacious.

Knocking on her door, I straighten my navy cardigan and brush through my hair with my fingers. Ingrid opens the door and gives me a huge smile, takes my hand, and says, "Come in, Emery. I'm so happy you're here, honey. You look beautiful. That navy cardigan looks impressive on you; it compliments your honey-colored hair perfectly."

"Thank you, Ingrid. You look amazing. I love how you're dressed casually, and those brown linen pants are great. You might get a bit cold, but don't worry—I put a blanket in the back seat.

"Well, aren't you thoughtful, Emery?" she says with a grin. "Are you ready?"

"Yes, how about you?"

"Almost; give me about five minutes, love. Come on and have a seat while you wait."

As Ingrid walks away, I can't help but watch her. I immediately notice her lovely hips, ass, and curves. My stomach fills with butterflies, and my feminine zone tenderly pulsates. Sitting on the sofa, I squirm a bit, trying to calm my feminine region, but all it is doing is spreading the ache.

"Damn, she is fine as hell," I whisper to myself. I stand up, trying to distract myself, but instead, I feel gravity pulling my wetness in my panties. "Damn," I mutter silently.

"I'm ready now, love, if you are," she says, approaching me looking like a million dollars and smelling like two.

I nod, feeling a bit bashful. Pushing my nerves aside, I open her door and say, "After you, Miss Mercer."

"You're too much, Miss Wilde," She says and giggles.

Driving down Highway 80, I glance over at Ingrid as she looks out at the Wilmington River as we cross it. We haven't spoken much during the drive; she seems to be taking in the lowcountry. Realizing she probably gets homesick at times, I've left her alone with her thoughts, allowing her to enjoy the scenery. I suppose even a huge star like Ingrid might possibly miss her roots and long for home.

"Thank you, Emery," she says sweetly as she looks at me.

"You're welcome, Ingrid, I'm enjoying spending time with you. There's no need to thank me."

She reaches for my hand, our fingers interlocking. She then turns her gaze back to the expansive marshlands and Lowcountry scenery. Swallowing a lump in my throat, I can't help but wonder what Ingrid wants from me, friendship, love or simply a companion to whom she can bare her soul. I'm unsure what she wants, but I know exactly what I want.

"Do you know the way from here, Emery?"

"Well, you might have to refresh my memory—I don't come out here often."

"Okay. Turn right up ahead."

Pulling up to her homeplace, I glance at her and watch her sparkling green eyes fill with tears. I stop the vehicle and turn it off. Taking her hand in mine, I whisper, "Are you okay, Ingrid?"

She smiles at me, then pulls my hands to her mouth and kisses them. "Well, I was until we arrived, Emery."

"How long has it been since you've been inside?"

"Four years," she whispers. I wait for her to process her homecoming before speaking again or leaving the Willys.

"Well, we might as well go inside," she says reluctantly.

Walking through the house, Ingrid starts to break down. I rush to her side. "Come here, Ingrid." She wraps her arms around my neck, giving me an intimate hug that shows her need for comfort. "It's okay, baby," I say to her. Maybe I shouldn't have called her that, but it felt right in the moment. Ingrid clings to me tightly, sobbing almost uncontrollably.

"Ingrid, let's sit on the couch. Come on, baby," I whisper, then gently release her and take her hand as we walk to the sofa and sit down. I pull her close, wrapping both arms around her as she continues to cry. As we sit together in this house full of memories, she begins to regain her composure.

"I'll be right back; I'm going to find some tissue."

Sitting back next to her, she smiles and laughs through her tears, "I didn't expect this, Emery. I'm not sure what I expected, but there's one thing I'm sure of," She says, then pauses.

"What's that, Ingrid?" I ask as I help dry her tears with tissue.

"I can't live here. It's too painful and full of ghosts."

"Come here," I whisper softly. Ingrid rests against my chest as I hold her. Overcome with another wave of emotions, she begins to weep. I hold on to her tightly, wishing for her pain to vanish. "Maybe you can't stay here, Ingrid, but that doesn't mean you can't move back to Savannah."

After a few moments, Ingrid stands and reaches for my hand. Taking her hand, I rise, and say, "Let's go, Emery. This is too much for me today."

As we head back into town, I keep my eyes on her, noting her somber mood. Not knowing how to help, I remain quiet but hold her hand, keeping our fingers interlaced, as I drive toward my warehouse.

"Are you taking me to *"The Wilde House?"*

"Yes, is that okay? I thought we could stop there. I'll make us lunch. Are you hungry?" She looks at me with her piercing green eyes, which I've watched a thousand times on the big screen at *The Strand Theatre* in Savannah.

Nodding, she says, "Yes, that would be lovely." She continues gazing at me, and I meet each gaze with a sincere smile. "You truly are a remarkable woman, Emery."

Feeling bold, I smile and give her a playful wink. She laughs, shaking her head, and I watch her dark curls bounce with each movement. I realize that the emotions I'm experiencing now are far more profound than anything my sixteen-year-old self could have ever imagined, let alone written about.

As I walk into the main entrance, my front salesperson approaches, her mouth dropping open in surprise. I laugh and say, "Ingrid, this is Isabelle Chase. Isabelle, this is…"

"Ingrid Mercer?" She says in disbelief.

"It's nice to meet you, Isabelle," Ingrid says sincerely.

Isabelle slaps me on the arm and says, "You never told me

you knew Ingrid Mercer! Why haven't you told me this, Emery?!"

I shrug and look at Ingrid, who is smiling at me. "I don't know. I guess I just didn't think about it. Anyway, we're heading to my loft for lunch. I won't be back at work until tomorrow. Okay?"

"Sure, Emery. I got it; don't worry," she says, still mesmerized by Ingrid.

Walking up the steps, Ingrid says, "She's cute, Emery." I glance at her and roll my eyes as we approach the top floor. "No comment?" she asks playfully.

Walking across the second floor to my loft, I say, "Well, there are three things completely wrong with your inquiry."

Walking into my loft apartment, I close the door, and Ingrid says, "And what are those three things?"

Laughing, I say, "Well, there are actually four things. One, she loves men. Two, she's my employee. Three, she's way too young. And the fourth, which is the most important, is that I am not attracted to her at all."

"Hmmm, " Ingrid mutters, then says with a playful smile, "Well, I'm just trying to get a sense of what your type is, Emery Wilde." She says this playfully.

Looking around my place, Ingrid says, "Emery, this loft is amazing. I absolutely love it. Show me around."

"Okay, but it's not that big. I wanted to leave most of my space for the business when I had this built."

"As you can see, this is the main area. I eat and lounge in here; it's where I spend most of my time when I'm not asleep. Over there is the bathroom." As we walk further back, I smell Ingrid's perfume. Her irresistible allure makes me feel slightly off balance. Leading her into the bedroom, I say, "This is obviously my bedroom."

Ingrid walks around my bedroom with her arms crossed

and a teasing grin. "Let me ask you something, Emery. If these walls could talk, what do you think they'd say?"

Blushing, I snicker and say, "You love to unnerve me, don't you?"

"Maybe," she replies with that same grin. "But you haven't answered my question," She adds as she sits on my bed. Oh damn, I think to myself. God, I'll never get this image out of my head—Ingrid, sitting on my bed.

"Well, these walls would whisper, 'Ingrid, I hate to break it to you, but Emery is very boring. All she does is work and sleep.'"

"You and your damn modesty, Emery Wilde," she says, rising and walking toward me. Ingrid walks past me and adds, "Maybe you need to give these walls something more interesting to talk about." She then exits my bedroom completely, leaving me standing there in erotic pain and wet again. "Dammit," I mutter.

CHAPTER SIX: INGRID

"Thank you for lunch, Emery; the salad was delicious. And this breeze is so refreshing," I say as I walk to the massive window and sit on the wide window sill.

"You're welcome Ingrid, "She says as she takes our dishes to the sink. I can't help but watch her as I sit feeling the coolness of the afternoon. Looking out the window, I look at downtown Savannah and begin to think. Could I really move home? Then I feel my eyes pooling with tears again as I recall walking through my childhood home earlier today.

I feel Emery's hand on my shoulder. I reach for it but my gaze stays fixed on Savannah. Emery sits on the opposite side of the window sill and watches me. "Are you okay, Ingrid?" she asks. I nod, but don't look at her. She knows I'm weeping again but understands I just need a minute.

Gazing back at her, I'm struck by her beauty, feeling both emotionally and sensually moved. Emery has stirred something in me since she picked me up at the airport, but now she's beginning to stir me sensually as well, it frightens me. Getting to know her and growing closer has been incredible, but these feelings are confusing. Emery is eighteen years younger than me. How could that possibly work? Why would she want a woman my age? Hollywood sure doesn't.

"Do you still feel up to driving to the beach tonight?" she asks

Turning towards her, I say, "Of course, Emery. You promised me a date at the beach."

"Oh, I know, but you've had an emotional day, so I wasn't sure," she says, reaching for my hand. I immediately grasp her hand, and our fingers interlock, finding their comfortable positions. Her touch feels different today; something has shifted within me. Gazing at her, I softly say, "I love being with you, Emery."

She meets my gaze but doesn't speak for a moment. Then she says, "Someone like you."

"Pardon me?" I ask.

"You said earlier that you wanted to know my type of woman." My eyes remain fixed on her haunting gray eyes. What is she trying to tell me? I stay silent but allowing my gaze to mingle with hers. This moment feels magical and ethereal, as if the twelve-year span has rapidly ushered in a new beginning for us.

"What are you really saying, Emery?"

Feeling the cool breeze blowing through this timeless and tender moment, I await her reply. Emery's gray eyes haunt me as I try to peer into her soul, wondering if she's held me there all these years.

She whispers, "You know what I'm saying, Ingrid."

Turning back toward Savannah, I ask, "Emery, how could that possibly work?"

"I have no idea, Ingrid. But I will tell you this," she says, pausing for me to look back at her. Turning toward her, she continues, "If I wrote you a note today, it would say the same thing, except I'm not young any longer, Ingrid."

"No, Emery, you're not, but we still have a significant age difference, love."

"Yes, I agree. We do.'" She then stands and reaches for my hand. "Would you like some Chardonnay?"

"That would be lovely, Emery." Walking to the couch, I realize everything has become so deep and complicated in an instant. Gazing at her, I see a remarkable and gorgeous woman I'd love to have in my life permanently, but that doesn't mean I'm entitled to her.

Emery sits on the couch with me, handing me a glass of wine, and we clink glasses without a proper toast. "I suppose this was bad timing after your breakdown earlier. I'm sorry."

"Emery, you have nothing to be sorry about, love. I adore you, and whatever is in your heart is important to me. I didn't realize that I was still there."

"You've remained there, Ingrid. Yes, there have been women in my life over the years, but they were all short-lived."

"Why is that, Emery? Please don't tell me it's because of me. You deserve a beautiful and remarkable woman like yourself."

"It's mainly because of this place, but I have thought about you a lot over the years and hoped you would come home and 'Find Me,' as mentioned in my note."

"I don't know what to say, Emery. Honey, could it be that you're simply star-struck?"

"Ingrid, I've known you my whole life. I admire your work. I've watched all of your movies, but when I look at you, I don't see the big movie star that everyone else sees. Sometimes, I feel goosebumps because I know you, but star-struck isn't what I feel for you, Ingrid."

"Well, that makes me happy. At least I know that's not the reason."

"What do you feel for me, Ingrid?"

"Hmmm, I utter, then take a sip of chardonnay. "Emery, if you asked me before you picked me up yesterday at the airport, before we spent that truly amazing evening and night together, I would have said: I love the young Emery, the one making her mark in this town. She's a genuine and pure soul who is also utterly gorgeous."

"Well, I'm asking you what you feel about this, Emery—the one sitting beside you right now."

As I move closer to Emery, I thread my fingers through a few strands of her lovely hair and kiss her cheek softly. "Emery, will you allow me some time to consider your question?"

"Yes, of course, Ingrid." She smiles sweetly at me while I feel her soft hair flowing through my fingers.

"Thank you. I'll have my answer for you tonight at the beach. You complicate my feelings, Emery. I need to process your question because you deserve a sincere and thoughtful response. I feel so many wonderful things about you, love."

"Emery, this is so invigorating!" I exclaim as she drives us up the Tybee Island shoreline on the packed sand. As we ride in Willys, I gaze at the sky in complete admiration. "The sky is so vivid and brilliant, love. And this cold January wind is exhilarating."

"Yes, it is. Hold on, Ingrid!" she shouts. Grabbing the top of the Jeep, I hang on, unsure of what's coming. Suddenly, Emery has Willys speeding through the water, the tires shooting vast streams of water back into the Ocean. I laugh with excitement and lean toward Emery, trying to stay dry.

I glance at Emery. She sweeps her hand through her hair, pushing it back as she peers out the windshield and laughs. At this moment, I realize the answer to her question. Look at her—so vibrant and free, so unencumbered. How could I help but be completely in love with her?

"Are you cold, Ingrid?"

"I'm freezing, but I don't give a damn. Keep driving." She looks at me and laughs, and then nods. We continue riding a few miles up the coast, watching the grandeur of the evening and enjoying life in the expansiveness of this beautiful seashore.

As we get closer to where we left the main road, Emery pulls into what looks like a hidden cove. Gazing at her, I feel my female core ache as I watch her shift the gears, maneuvering the Jeep into the secluded spot. She turns off the Willys and looks at me. "Well, did that cure your need for speed tonight, Miss Mercer"?

I immediately suck in my cheeks, fighting the urge to laugh like a silly girl. "I believe I got my money's worth, Miss Wilde."

"Good!" she says with a laugh as she jumps out of the Jeep. "I like for my customers to have a favorable experience."

"You're hilarious, Emery." As I get out of the Jeep, I notice the light fading quickly. Teasingly, I ask, "Is this where you bring your women?"

She doesn't miss a beat and quickly replies, "No, I take them to North Beach."

Laughing, I say, "I guess I deserved that." She looks at me and nods. "By the way, what are you doing?"

"I'm freezing, and I know you are too, so I'm going to build us a fire."

"Really? Oh, this will be so much fun. Damn, woman, you're a romantic. I should have known." She glances at me and grins as she drops the wood on the ground.

Emery has a wonderful fire going within a few moments, and then spreads a large wool blanket in front of it. "Come on, let's get warm," she says with a smile.

Sitting on the blanket beside Emery in front of the warm, glowing fire, I feel free and light. "Emery, spending time with you has been amazing. I don't know when I've had a better time coming home."

Emery moves closer to me. "Good, I love being with you, Ingrid. You're so much fun."

"More fun than your young ones?" I ask playfully.

She looks at me, rolls her eyes again, and says, "Ingrid, there are no others. I am a free and single woman." She bumps against me and then adds, "Are you wanting me to admit that I have someone, or are you just reassuring yourself that I am indeed free?"

"Damn, Emery. You sure do shoot straight, honey." I look into the fire and add, "I like that about you. It's a rare quality."

"Are you getting warm?" she asks.

"Yes, this fire feels so nice, thank you." As I peer into the flames, I think about being here on the Atlantic coast, where my roots are. "I'm over two thousand miles from my life in California, Emery. And I don't miss it one bit."

"Would you miss it over time if you moved back?"

"I don't know. That life lacks real friends, so it's not really a life. It's more of a career." I think about some of my friends out there for a moment. Many of my actor colleagues are transitioning into television, hoping that will sustain them as they age. Still, I'm not sure if I want that."

"Ingrid, may I say something?"

Pulling my knees up to my body, I wrap my arms around them and lay my head sideways to look at Emery. "Of course."

"When I look at you, I don't see a woman whose time on the screen is fading. I see a beautiful and vibrant woman with intense passion. You have a bright light and fire inside of you, Ingrid Mercer. The lights of Hollywood may be shining on younger stars now, but your light shines outward and burns hot and constant; that isn't something I see in many women, Ingrid."

"Emery, my love," I whisper. With my knees still drawn up close to my body, I put my forehead on them and begin to weep again. Emery moves next to me, holds me close, and hugs me. Her body next to me is comforting yet it also stirs me sensually as well as emotionally.

I pull away, turn toward her, and gaze into her haunting gray eyes, which twinkle in the firelight. I reach for her hands, and we interlock our fingers. "You're so gorgeous in this light, Emery." Looking at her hands, I glance back into her eyes and whisper, "I still can't answer your question properly, but Emery, I'm willing to give us a chance if you want me."

I see tears pooling in Emery's eyes as I continue to look at this beautiful woman that I indeed want. "Come away with me, Emery."

"To where, Ingrid?" I pull her hand to my lips, and I kiss it while gazing into her eyes. I close my eyes, inhale her scent, and kiss her hand again.

"I don't know, Emery, but we can't do this here in Savannah. And after today at the house, I want to run away from that."

"So, are we running away? Or what exactly are we doing?"

"No, my love. That came out all wrong." I cup Emery's cheek and add, "We won't be running away. We will be exploring our feelings for each other."

"Ingrid," she whispers. I watch her sweet face, waiting for her answer. My heart races as I feel myself falling into her deep gray eyes as she watches me. "When did you think of this?"

"After you asked me that question today. I've Wanted to travel by train across the country for a long time. I've spent the last decade stuck on sound stages, and not experiencing the real world."

"I'm not asking you to travel with me as a friend, Emery. I want to be open and honest about why I'm inviting you to go with me." Grabbing a stick, I turn toward the fire and begin poking it, allowing the flames to grow.

Turning back to Emery, I say, "I'm simply too scared to answer your question because what I feel for you is over-whelming. I'm frightened enough just taking this chance with you."

CHAPTER SEVEN: EMERY

"I'm terrified too, Ingrid. Being with you has been absolutely incredible, and while I've enjoyed every moment of our playful flirting, I need you to know that my feelings for you are deep and genuine. Do you have any idea how hard it was sleeping next to you last night? Restraining myself was an immeasurable task."

Ingrid snuggles close, resting her chin on my shoulder and whispers, "It would have been amazing, Emery."

"Are you flirting with me, or are you being serious?"

Ingrid pulls away, looks at me, and says, "Both. You know I'm a flirt—I always have been. But I wouldn't flirt with you like this, Emery if I didn't have feelings for you. That would be cruel, considering our history."

She tosses the stick she's been poking the fire with into it and says, "It would have been an honor making love to you all night Emery Wilde. Your charm and allure have unexpectedly swept me off my feet. If you can't see that, then you're a damn fool."

"Ingrid!"

"What?!" She snaps, rising to her feet and crossing her

arms. She gazes intently into the fire. I rise and stand next to her. She lifts her eyes to me, and I give her a grin.

"Do you remember the last thing you said to me last night before you said goodnight?" She looks at me quizzically. I pull her closer. "You said, '*Obviously, you don't realize what a catch you are, Miss Wilde.*'" I gaze into her feisty green eyes and grin. "Obviously, I don't know that, Ingrid, but you're helping me to believe it."

She starts to smile at me. With a grin, I ask, "I need a hug; can you help me with that?"

Ingrid puts her arms around my neck, and I pull her close, encircling her waist. After a moment, I move my hand down towards her ass and watch her green eyes grow sultry.

Leaning into her, our lips meet. Ingrid's lips are tender and moist, warm from the fire. Feeling my lust for her churn, I keep my hands on her ass and grip it. Ingrid opens her mouth, inviting me inside. Her tongue is warm, soft, and erotically spicy. Leaving one hand on her ass, the other travels up her back to her dark curls. Threading my fingers through her hair, I pull her to me fiercely, wanting her to feel my desire for her, my lust, my hunger. Our tongues swirl and dance with the fire that burns in my gut and on the beach. Though she's tried to break our kiss twice, I hold her tightly, unwilling to release her until I'm satisfied she understands my desire and what I want from her.

She runs her fingers through the back of my hair with both hands, gripping a few strands tightly. Pulling away slightly, she looks into my eyes. "My god, Emery! I had no idea you were this passionate!"

Holding her close, I whisper, "When do you want to leave?"

"Tonight," she replies, then dives back into my mouth, clearly craving more. After several passionate kisses, I release her mouth and hungrily kiss her neck, eager to please that sweet erogenous zone. "Emery," she whispers. "Honey, we need to stop for a minute."

Releasing her, I pull away, giving her space while gazing at her in the firelight. "Okay, you're right," I say, "but it's incredibly hard, Ingrid"

She whispers, "I know baby," then grips my hair again, pulling me back for more. Ingrid releases her passion for me, and I feel myself becoming wet and on the verge of an orgasm.

Holding the woman I've longed for since my teenage years, I give in, allowing myself to explore her allure and complexity. As I feed on her, I yearn for more. Moving my hand to her breast, grasping her bosoms in my hand. Immediately, I slide my hand under her sweater to feel her better. As I trace the outline of her bra tenderly, she moans into my mouth. Desperate for more, I reach behind, unhooking her brassiere as she tugs at my hair, her desire for me growing more insistent.

My hands return to her bosoms and I cup them gently, brushing my thumbs across her nipples to feel their erectness. Ingrid pulls away to look at me. Holding her gaze, I continue brushing her nipples as she stares at me in disbelief. Rolling her nipples between my finger and thumb, I watch her face.

"Emery," She whispers breathlessly; she touches my face, allowing me to continue loving her. Holding her breasts, I lift them and gaze at her, enjoying her reaction to my touch.

Brushing her nipples again, looking deeply into her, I whisper, "Does this feel good, baby?"

"You have no idea what you're doing to me, Emery."

"Why don't you tell me, Ingrid," I whisper, as I continue holding her on the edge.

"Emery, love, we need to stop—you're the only one with the power to do that now."

"Why do we need to stop, Ingrid?" She closes her eyes and moans. She looks back at my lips muttering, "I've noticed your pouty, sensual lips for years."

"You could have kissed them anytime you wanted to. You know that."

Ingrid nods as she looks back at them. "I'm glad I waited, but you would have tasted just as sweet back then, baby."

"Oh god, Ingrid, I've ached for you for years," I say as I tug at her nipples.

"Emery, baby. We must stop. You're the one in control right now, so please, baby." I hear her words, but I feel as helpless as she does. Closing my eyes, I reluctantly release her as she's asked. Taking her in my arms, I hug her tenderly.

"Okay, baby. I'll stop for now."

"Thank you, Emery. But honey, that wasn't what I wanted."

Pulling away, I look at her and smile. "Turn around, and let me re-hook your brassiere."

"You're incredible, Emery," she says, turning her head towards me as I work on her brassiere. You have a fire in you that I didn't see coming."

As I finish with her brassiere, I grin, and wrap my arms around her from behind. "And you are even hotter than my fantasies of you."

"Hmmm," she says as she turns back to face me. "Will you tell me all of your fantasies about me?"

Nodding with a grin, I say, "Only if you will relive them with me."

Pulling away, she says, "Your last name suits you, Emery." We both laugh. "Dear god, does that name indeed fit you. You're a damn animal, girl."

"Well, you got half of that right, Ingrid." She looks at me oddly. "I'm not a girl, but with you, I am definitely a fucking animal."

"Is it too late to call this off?" She asks playfully.

Glancing at my watch, I nod and say, "Yes, that ended approximately twenty-six hours ago when I picked you up at the airport.

Ingrid laughs loudly, steps off the blanket, and kicks some sand at me. "Damn you, Emery Wilde. I came home for a nice visit to simply clear up Mama's estate, and now here I am at night on the beach, my whole body on fire for you." She runs her fingers through her hair and lets out a light scream at the fire.

"Ingrid, I know you're not sorry this has happened, but please answer me seriously."

Crossing her arms, she looks at me and asks, "What, Emery?"

"Do you wish to continue? I need to know, Ingrid." She walks over, wraps an arm around my waist, cups my cheek, and looks me in the eyes.

"Yes, Emery, I want you. I was just being a bit dramatic and trying to lighten things up. But, honey, we have a lot to decide before diving into this."

"Such as?" I ask.

She takes my hand and says, "Emery, we need to tell Lillian. I cannot and will not embark on a romantic relationship with her daughter without her knowing."

"And what if she's opposed to it?"

Ingrid releases my hand, folds her arms again and says, "Well, I didn't say I need her approval. I said I won't do this without her knowing that you and I are romantically involved."

Looking at the fire, I sigh. "You're right, Ingrid. She needs to know. I'll tell her."

"Oh no, honey!" she says firmly. "This is for me to do. I must be woman enough to ask her for your hand, so to speak, Emery." She looks at me and adds, "It might involve her knowing about the letter you gave me years ago."

"Ingrid, I don't care if she knows about that now."

"Emery, that note is very special to me. I'll only tell her about it if I have to. I hope it doesn't come to that, because your love letter is the one tangible thing in my life that has remained pure and innocent."

Watching Ingrid as the firelight dances across her, I smile. "That's beautiful, Ingrid."

"It's true, Emery."

"I always hoped you'd come home and *'find me,'* Ingrid."

CHAPTER EIGHT: INGRID

As Emery drives me to the hotel, she shifts gears intermittently, but after each shift, she grabs my hand. It makes me smile and feel giddy like a schoolgirl. But thinking about talking to Lillian fills my heart with dread. I don't know how to tell her about my feelings for Emery. God, I don't want to lose my best friend. But I'm not walking away from Emery if she disapproves.

We stop at the front entrance, and Emery leaves her Willys running. I look at her, wink, and smile. "Darling, I can't see you again until I've spoken with Lillian."

She nods and asks, "When will that be?"

I reach for a few strands of her hair and tuck them behind her ear. "Hopefully tomorrow. Your Mama has invited me to the house for dinner on Friday night, but I'm not sure if that will happen."

"Okay, Ingrid." She turns toward me and adds, "Maybe it would be better if we talk to her together."

Shaking my head, I say, "Emery, I appreciate your concern, but I'm a big girl, and I want her truthful reaction. I don't believe she will be completely honest with me if you're there. Do you understand?"

"It sounds like it might get ugly, Ingrid."

"I'm hoping not, but knowing how protective she is of her children, especially you, I need to be prepared for that."

I kiss her on the cheek and whisper, "Call me when you get in bed."

Emery's eyes light up, and she grins at me shyly, "I will, Ingrid. I promise." She winks and then speeds off in her Willys. My heart feels full, and I suddenly feel twenty years younger.

Lillian meets me at *Old Towne Café* the next morning around ten o'clock. We sit in the same booth as yesterday and order brunch. "Thank you for inviting me, Ingrid. Is something wrong? You seem unsettled."

"I'm nervous, Lillian," I say, looking into her gray eyes— the same gray eyes that Emery has.

"I never noticed until now that Emery has your eyes, Lillian."

Grinning, she says, "Yes, she does. I like to think she has a lot of me in her."

Sipping my coffee, I continue gazing into the same haunting eyes I've loved for the last two days, "She has a lot of you in her, Lillian."

Lillian smiles and then looks at me oddly. "Are you okay, Ingrid?

"Not really, Lillian. I have something to talk with you about that is sensitive, something that could be life-altering."

Stirring her coffee, she gazes at me, searching for a clue. "Well, talk to me, Ingrid."

"I don't know where to start, but let me say this first.

When I went to Mama's house yesterday, I was a complete mess when I left. I realize that I can't handle that right now."

"Well, Ingrid, there's no rush, honey. Is there?"

"No, there isn't. I've decided to take a train trip across the country, maybe all the way to San Francisco."

Oh gosh, that sounds great, Ingrid. When did you decide this?"

"Well, It's something I've thought about doing for a long time. Since January is slow for me, I've decided to go this month."

"That sounds amazing. Ingrid, you've worked nonstop for years; it will do you good. But wouldn't you rather go abroad? There's a big world out there."

Laughing, I say, "I'm aware of that, and you know I've traveled abroad some. But now I feel the need to see this wonderful, raw country of ours before I explore elsewhere."

"We do have a beautiful country, Ingrid. I find that admirable."

Sipping my coffee, I say, "I've asked Emery to come with me."

Lillian gives me a puzzled expression. "What did she say?"

"Well, she said, 'Yes.'"

"She did?" Lillian looks away, lost in thought. "That's odd; she's basically married to that warehouse. She's a workaholic like you, so it might do her some good to let go and enjoy life for a bit."

"Lillian, there is more. But I need you to promise me something, okay?"

Lillian gives me a blank, apprehensive stare. "Promise what?"

"You will sit here and keep talking to me and not walk away, no matter what."

She furrows her brow and says, "I don't have a clue what

you're talking about, but okay, I promise I'll stay here and discuss whatever's on your mind, Ingrid."

"Okay, good." I swallow hard and begin "Ingrid, are you aware that Emery has had a crush on me since she was a teenager?"

Lillian giggles and says, "Of course I am, Ingrid." She covers her mouth with her hand and asks, "Has Emery made a pass at you?"

"Well, no, Lillian."

"Ingrid, just tell me what you're trying to say, especially if it involves Emery."

"Lillian, Emery is coming with me on this trip so she and I can explore our feelings for one another. I love her, Lillian. You may hate me, but I love her so very much."

"Ingrid! My god! You didn't just say that to me!" I sit quietly, observing her reaction. Her eyes begin to glisten. My heart twists with pain as I watch my best friend from childhood become completely disappointed and, likely, disgusted with me.

The waiter sets our food down and then leaves. Lillian pushes her plate aside, turns away from me, crosses her legs, and begins grinding her teeth. "God damn you, Ingrid Mercer. That's my child you're playing with."

"I know, Lillian. I am well aware that she's your daughter, but I assure you I'm not playing."

"Ingrid, I can't discuss this any further until I speak with Emery."

"Okay, but please don't end things between us. I love you, Lillian. I always have. Please don't let me lose you."

"How did this happen, Ingrid?"

"Are you still willing to talk a while longer? It might take some time, and I don't want you storming out on me."

Lillian is still grinding her teeth behind that same perfect jaw that Emery has. "Yes, I'll sit here and talk with you. I'm shocked and mad as hell at you, but I want to understand how this happened. Go ahead, Ingrid."

"Before I begin, I want to remind you of one thing."

"What?" She asks sternly.

"Emery is a twenty-eight-year-old woman who's slept with other women, Lillian."

"Please don't tell me you and Emery have slept together, Ingrid." she pleads, holding her hand to her head.

"No, we haven't, Lillian."

"Thank god!" She responds.

I want to say, *'But we will,'* since she acts like that would totally disgust her. Instead, I take a deep breath, understanding that I'm just not who she envisioned for her daughter.

"Ingrid, I know Emery prefers women. I'm aware of that, even though we've never discussed it. She's my child, and I know her."

Lillian looks at me but then, reluctantly, turns to face me fully. She picks up her coffee and then meets my gaze.

"Thank you," I say and smile. "I want to tell you about something that happened at the big party you threw for me in Savannah twelve years ago to celebrate my Oscar win."

She nods and says, "Okay, I'm listening."

Looking away, I picture my sweet Emery. "At one point in the night, I stepped outside for fresh air and I sat on a column. Emery came over to me." Lillian keeps her eyes fixed on me, listening intently."

"As she approached me, I smiled, hugged her, and asked her if she was bored. She laughed and replied, *'No, I could never be bored around you, Ingrid.'*" As I recount this to Lillian, a smile begins to form on my face, but I try to stay focused.

"Then what happened, Ingrid?"

Looking into Lillian's eyes, I say, "She handed me a note and told me, *'Read this later, Ingrid, when the party ends.'*" I did indeed read her sweet note when I went to bed that night." Touching my clutch, I add, "That note has remained in my wallet since that night, Lillian."

She leans back and asks, "What did the note say?"

"The note is too pure and tender for me to share in its entirety. But it was a love poem that ended with, *'When your heart is free, find me, for though I am young, I'll wait for you patiently.'*"

Ingrid, that's just a love note from a sixteen-year-old girl with a huge crush on a thirty-four-year-old actress. You can't possibly think of it in any other way."

"I never have, Lillian. The note has brought me a lot of comfort over the years. Whenever I was feeling down or needed a reminder of home, I;d read Emery's note repeatedly. It always grounded me in some way.

"Lillian, when Emery picked me up at the airport, I was immediately captivated by her. She's an absolutely stunning woman now. We went to the hotel, and had so much fun that night, laughing until one a.m. with nothing at all inappropriate happening.

"Keep going, Ingrid," she says, her eyes on me as her food remains untouched.

"Yesterday, I broke down at Mama's house, and Emery was incredibly tender with me. We went to her loft for a salad and talked, and last night, we ended up on the beach and kissed. Lillian, somehow, within a period of twenty-four hours, Emery and I fell in love."

"Damn," she says deflated.

"I can't explain it. Maybe the note and Emery's unchanged love for me laid the foundation for our love. All I know is that I love Emery, and I'll never deny it. She's a remarkable woman, and I want her in my life. And that's what she wants, too."

Lillian shakes her head, remaining silent.

"I told her last night when she dropped me off in front of the hotel that I couldn't see her again until I spoke with you about us. So here I am, with my heart laid bare before you." We both sit silently for a few moments. "Thank you for not walking out on me."

Resting her fist against her face as it leans on the table, Lillian nods, lifts her eyes to mine, and asks, "When will the two of you leave?"

"In a few days, I suppose."

"Ingrid. I'm going to leave now. I have to swallow and digest this somehow. And yes, I know that Emery is a grown woman who's had intimate relations with other women. I imagined one of them would be my daughter-in-law, so to speak, but never in a million years did I ever think it would be you."

Lillian rises, flicks her keys, then walks to my side. I look up as she gazes down at me. She touches my face and says, "I still love you, Ingrid. Thank you for coming and telling me this. Most people wouldn't have been this brave or forthright." She kisses my forehead and then turns to leave.

CHAPTER NINE: EMERY

Walking through my antique warehouse, I see Mom approaching with a somewhat intense expression. "Hi Mom. What are you doing here?"

"Emery, can we go to your loft and talk?" she asks with a serious tone.

"Sure, come on." I can tell from her expression that she knows. She must have come straight here after speaking with Ingrid.

Mom and I walk into my loft. I ask, "Can I get you something to drink, Mama?"

"Emery, you haven't called me Mama in years. You're clearly aware that I've spoken with Ingrid. I know you too well. Please explain to me how this has happened."

Sitting on the couch, I look at her and say, "Because I love her, Mama. I always have, and she makes me happy. Sure, when I was younger, it was probably just a teenage crush."

"Emery, Ingrid could practically be your Mother. Honey, Ingrid is a beautiful and very appealing woman, but she's eighteen years older than you."

"Mom, men do it all the time. Why can't an older woman fall in love with someone younger?"

"Because women have stricter boundaries, Emery! And *you're* my daughter!"

"Fair enough, Mom, but this is more on me than Ingrid."

"What do you mean?" she asks, looking startled.

"I've pursued her. It wasn't the other way around. Somehow, in my pursuit, I caught her attention. Mama, I love Ingrid. I want this with her. I've always loved her. I'll admit, women my age don't appeal to me. They never have."

"Have you been with other older women, Emery?"

"Yes, I have."

"Who? I want to know what other older women you've been with. Is it women here in Savannah?"

"I'm not going to share those details with you. It would serve no purpose. I'm only telling you this so you will know that Ingrid isn't my first older woman."

"Emery, I just don't understand."

"Mom, you don't have to understand it. But you need to find a way to be okay with us, because if you aren't, it could never work for Ingrid and me."

"Well, since you're going away together, what I say is of little consequence."

"You're right. We would still go away together, but it would be doomed, and my happiness would be shattered. If you can't find a way to accept this, Ingrid and I could never work, and I don't know what that might do to me, Mama."

Feeling a painful rawness in my heart, I begin to cry. Mama pulls me in her arms, and I lean against her. My tears flow uncontrollably from my soul. "Mama, please, I can't lose Ingrid, and I don't want to lose you either."

"Well, honey. You would never lose me."

"Yes, I could, Mama. If you can't give your blessing, then Ingrid and I won't have a future together—our love will die, and things between you and me would never be the same. Mama, you've always understood me, and I know you feel something with me that you don't with the others."

"You're right about that, Em. Honey, you've always seemed to love me deeper than the others, and you've always made that very clear. You've always made me feel incredibly special."

"You are, Mama. I couldn't have asked for a better parent than you."

Mama holds me for a long while, threading her fingers slowly through my hair as she's done since I was a child. "I love you, Emery. I'll find a way to open my heart for this, baby."

Sitting up, I see the immense love in her eyes and lean in to kiss her on the lips. She looks at me and laughs. "Emery, that is the first time in your life you have ever kissed me on the lips. You must really have it bad for Ingrid."

I shake my head and say, "Mama, I've always loved her. But now I know, without a doubt, that I'm in love with her." I glance at Mama's eyes, and she nods, looking down.

"Okay, Emery. Before this, I had already invited Ingrid over for dinner on Friday. Will you come too?"

Hugging her, I say, "Yes! Thank you, Mama."

Continuing to hug me, she asks, "Emery, will you please do me one favor?"

Pulling away, I look at her and nod.

"Will you please start calling me Mama again? I hate "MOM!"

Smiling, I say, "I sure will, Mama!"

"Thank god. I don't know when you became too big to stop calling me that. I'm a Southern lady, honey, and we are called "Mama."

∽

Picking up my phone, I take a deep breath and dial the Savannah Hotel.

"Hello, this is the Savannah Hilton. How may we assist you?"

"This is Miss Wilde calling for Miss Mercer in room 213."

"One moment, please," the gentleman on the line says.

Ingrid answers, "Hello."

"I need to see you, baby."

"Oh, Emery, honey. I'm aching for you; I need to see you, too. Have you spoken with your Mama?"

I take a deep breath and say, "Yes, she left a few minutes ago. How did she respond to you, Ingrid?"

"At first not very well, but she appreciated me telling her how I feel about you, face-to-face, and what my intentions are."

"I know that had to be very hard for you," I say, settling onto the sofa.

"Yes, it was, Emery. But, I'd sit and talk with the devil himself if it meant being with you."

"Damn, Ingrid, you're an incredible woman," I say, smiling, "When can I see you?"

"Now." She says with a giggle.

I laugh and say, "That's not soon enough."

"Emery Wilde, you are something else. Will you come over?"

"Yes, let me change, and I'll be there within a half hour."

"Okay, baby. I'll see you then. Bye, love."

"Bye, Ingrid."

Knocking on Ingrid's door, my heart races just like it did yesterday. When she opens the door, I see the woman I love more than anything on this earth. She reaches out for me with both hands and pulls me inside.

Immediately, we're locked in a torrid, unmovable kiss. My hungry soul aches to engulf my new love as I embrace her. As our kisses ignite, my hands begin to travel, searching lustfully for her perfect ass.

Ingrid has her hands in my thick hair, grabbing it, and pulling closer. Her touch and tongue are driving me to the edge. An intense restricting ache burns through every nerve ending I have, radiating mercilessly to my sacred sanctuary. I'm restraining myself from ripping her clothes off and pulling her to the bed we shared two nights ago—the night my feminine soul pulsed mercilessly, craving her smell and taste.

She pulls away, stepping back. "My god, Emery. We need to slow down or at least talk about this, baby."

"I agree, Ingrid, but we can't possibly wait much longer."

"Come and sit with me, Emery," she says, reaching out her hand for mine.

Sitting down, I say, "Ingrid, I've never been like this with anyone before. You drive me wild. My god, how I crave you."

"Emery, honey. I believe that. You're such a genteel woman., and I am too. But somehow when we're together we're explosive."

"Yes, we are. I know we need to slow this down, but I don't know how Ingrid."

"Well, why don't you take me on a proper date. I'd love that, Emery."

Grinning, I say, "I'd love that, too." I stand and walk out of her hotel room, shutting the door behind me as I grin. I knock again and hear her ask, "Who is it?"

"This is Miss Wilde, I'm here to pick up Miss Mercer for lunch." Opening the door again, she smiles and giggles, saying, "Please come in, Miss Wilde."

"Thank you, Miss Mercer. Are you ready for our date, or do you need a few minutes?"

"Please have a seat, Emery. I'll only be a minute." She walks into the bathroom. I sit down, trying my hardest not to break into laughter.

She comes out looking like a million bucks and walks over to me. I offer her my hand with a grin. "Aren't you a perfect lady, Miss Wilde?"

"I'm trying my best, Miss Mercer," I say with a playful smile. "I hope you don't mind riding in my Willys Jeep. The only other option is to drive to my Mama's and borrow her Packard."

Ingrid looks at me like I've lost my marbles and says, "The Willys will be just fine."

"Let's go," I say, then kiss her cheek.

Smiling at me, she says, "Oh, Emery, why in the hell do you want a woman my age?"

"I don't want a woman your age," I reply. She looks at me curiously, and I add, "I want you, Ingrid Mercer."

"Damn, Emery. You've always been charming, honey, but now you have it in spades. Take me wherever you'd like, baby."

Sitting on the Veranda at The Seaside Café back on Tybee Island, Ingrid and I enjoy this crisp January day. The wind is cool and brisk as we continue sipping on the last of our bottle of Pinot Noir. It catches Ingrid's dark hair, blowing it sensually and freely. "You have the most beautiful hair, Ingrid."

She grins and winks at me. "Thank you, Emery, that's very sweet, love."

"Emery, how long can you be away from *The Wilde House?*

Please be honest. I want us to embark on this transcontinental train trip with clear and realistic expectations."

"Let me ask you this, Ingrid: Where do you want our final destination to be?"

"Well, when I've been planning this in my head over the past few years, my destination has always been San Francisco."

"How much time did you allot for that?" I ask, taking a sip of my wine while my gaze lingers on her exotic green eyes, which burn with passion for me.

Well, after I reached San Francisco, I planned to return to my home in Hollywood Hills. I figured that with the stops I wanted to make along the way, it might take about two weeks.

"Two weeks with you would be amazing, Ingrid. And January isn't very busy for me, so this is a perfect time to leave."

Ingrid reaches for my hands, our fingers interlocking. We share an infectious smile. "Emery, we could fly back to Savannah after the trip. We'll likely be tired of the train by then, so that would be the most logical option"

Gazing at her, I suddenly feel somber, and I look out at the waves crashing onto the shore. "Emery, what's wrong, baby?"

"I just got scared for a moment."

"Why, love?"

Pulling away gently, I look into her eyes and ask, "What about us after the trip? Will you move back to Savannah, Ingrid?"

"Emery, before we started this, I told you the other night that I was tired of my life and career and thinking about moving home. Mama's house is too haunted, but you were right; that doesn't mean I can't move back to Savannah."

"You wouldn't break my heart, would you, Ingrid?"

Gazing into my eyes, she touches my cheek and asks, "Will you please take me back to the secluded cove we went to before?"

Standing, I reach for her hand, and she takes it. We walk to the Willys.

Pulling into the remote cove, I drive and park under a canopy of vines and overhanging branches, then turn off the Jeep. We sit in silence, holding hands, listening to the waves breaking and the seagulls chirping and grunting.

Turning towards her, I see her green eyes welling with tears. "Ingrid," I whisper.

"I have the answer to your question now, Emery." As I help her dry her eyes, my heart sinks. I know she cares for me, but I'm so scared. "I just realized something."

"What, Ingrid?"

Shaking her head as she continues crying, she says, "I told Lillian how I feel about you before I told you. That's backward, isn't it?"

Feeling better, I touch her face and ask, "What did you tell her?"

Ingrid finishes drying her eyes, then tosses the tissue onto the dash and looks at me. "Emery Wilde, somehow, between you picking me up at the airport and dropping me off last night, you've completely bewitched and enchanted me."

Ingrid's green eyes hold mine as she cups my cheek and says, "Emery, I'm in love with you, baby."

At her words, my heart and body reach a climax in a whirlwind of joy that overwhelms me. I collapse into her lap, tears streaming down my cheeks as I hold onto her tightly

Ingrid lies against me and asks, "Emery, how could you not have known I'm completely in love with you?"

Breathlessly, I whisper, "I knew, but I wasn't sure you'd tell me. I've loved you for so long, Ingrid." Hugging her tighter, I add, "Hearing those words from you has left me reeling, my heart aching with overwhelming joy."

Threading her fingers through my hair, I calm down with her touch. "Baby, I'm sorry if I've scared you; that wasn't my intention. I had no idea this would affect you like this. Damn, you really do love me, Emery."

Rising, I look at her with tearful eyes and a smile. Ingrid grips the back of my hair, gazes into my soul, and whispers, "I'm so in love with you, Emery Wilde."

"I'm in love with you, Ingrid," I whisper to her. She touches my lips tenderly and sweetly.

"My sweet Emery," she whispers against my lips as she holds my face.

"Stay with me forever, Ingrid." She looks at me, nods softly, and smiles.

"Yes, my love. You are what I want my next twenty years and more to look like." Tenderly, she kisses my cheek and whispers, "You're so beautiful, Emery. You always have been."

"Ingrid, I've always loved you. I'm so happy that you came home to *'Find Me.'*"

"Somehow, my heart knew it was time, Emery. This isn't a coincidence."

CHAPTER TEN: INGRID

"Lillian, this dinner was amazing. You've always been an excellent cook, honey."

"Thank you, Ingrid. It was just a simple meal, but I'm glad you enjoyed it," she says, sipping her wine.

"I've always enjoyed sitting with you on your back patio. How many problems have we solved on this porch through the years, Lillian?"

Lillian laughs and says, "Well, I'm not sure if we actually solved any, but we damn sure tried."

We laugh together. Although the evening has been strained, Lillian has treated me with her usual kindness and love.

Emery enters the back patio and smiles at me. "Emery, honey, will you bring the bottle of chardonnay from the kitchen counter and get yourself a glass?"

"Okay, Mama."

Lillian grins at me and says, "One very positive thing has come from all of this—Emery is calling me Mama again instead of Mom."

Laughing, I say, "I'll make sure that never changes, Lillian," and give her a wink. She looks at me, then glances away.

"I know this is hard for you, Lillian. Thank you for keeping this dinner date with me."

"Oh, hush, Ingrid. I'm glad it's just the three of us. I was going to invite the whole family, but after this week, I wanted it to be just the three of us. I sent Ted to his brother's house so the three of us could have some privacy."

Emery returns with the wine and pours another glass for Lillian and me. She looks at me, winks, and then sits down. "Mama, thank you for dinner tonight."

Lillian smiles at her tenderly. "Emery, honey, you don't have to thank me; I love cooking for you." Emery nods and takes a sip of her wine.

"Mama, Ingrid, and I are leaving Sunday morning and will be gone for about two weeks."

She looks at us both and asks, "How are you going to take this cross-country trip and remain unseen, Ingrid? It's easier when you come here because the town respects your privacy, but traveling across the country, you might be hounded by photographers and reporters."

"That's true. But over the past few days, we've made all our reservations in Emery's name, and I'm pretty good at dressing down to avoid the press and fans."

Lillian leans in and says, "This is still a bit much for me, but Emery, I see how happy Ingrid makes you." She leans back, gazes at me, takes a deep breath, and giggles.

"Why are you giggling, Mama?" Emery asks.

Gazing at me, she continues laughing and says, "Well, over the years, Ingrid, you've shared your love interests with me." She laughs a bit harder and adds, "But, honey, I've never seen you this smitten and enchanted before. You clearly adore Emery."

I smile and laugh, then ask Emery to step out of the room

briefly. After she leaves, I walk to Lillian and sit on the foot-stool in front of her. She looks me in the eyes. "Lillian, I'd die for Emery. I will always protect and love her, honey. Please know this." She nods at me.

"You make Emery happy. What more can a parent want, Ingrid?"

"Do you still love me the same, Lillian?"

Leaning in, she says, "Yes, Ingrid. This is all new, but I could never stop loving you, honey. I know you'll love and protect Emery." I touch her face and nod.

"Is it safe for me to come back in?" Emery says from the entryway. Lillian and I laugh. Rising, I reach out to Emery. She takes my hand, holds my gaze, and smiles."

Glancing back at Lillian, her eyes meet mine. We share an intimate look, and she nods and winks at me, "Thank you, Lillian."

Sunday 8:00 a.m.

"Are you ready, baby?" I whisper in Emery's ear as we board the train. She winks at me and brushes her face against my hair. Closing my eyes, I feel her immense love and a million butterflies gathering in my stomach. Taking her hand, the butterflies flutter through my heart and soul, serenading me with a tender melody. Feeling warm tears, I clasp Emery's hand and glance at her. She smiles at me and whispers softly, "I love you."

With fingers intertwined, we wait to board. "I absolutely love your hair up like this, Ingrid. It's sexy as hell, but I can't wait to take it down tonight."

"Emery, you are wrecking my panties. Dammit."

Snickering, she whispers, "I'm sorry baby. I'll take those down tonight as well." Looking at her, I roll my eyes and shake my head.

"Hush, dammit. There are dozens of people around us. Putting my hair up and wearing sunglasses are part of my disguise. What do you think?"

Emery looks at me and smiles. "People are still going to stare at you, gorgeous, but I don't think they'll realize it's you."

"Good, that makes me happy. The beautiful scenery and you are all I wish to interact with on this trip. That was a great idea, reserving everything in your name, Miss Wilde." She grins and winks at me.

Finding our private compartment, Emery and I sit comfortably, waiting for the breakfast we ordered after boarding. "This trip is already magical, Ingrid."

Tucking a few strands of her hair behind her ear, I gaze into her eyes and say, "You being with me makes it magical, Emery." She smiles, then snuggles against my neck and bites it playfully.

"Oh, god. Emery, honey, please don't start that." I say with laughter.

"Yes, ma'am. I'll try to be the genteel lady you say I am," she says with a grin.

"Well, honey, definitely in public, but I love your playful, wicked side, baby. It's raw and untamed." I say, shaking my head at her.

"Are you going to try to tame me, Miss Mercer?"

"Emery, honey. I have no intentions of ever taming you."

"Good, I don't wish to tame you either."

"Hello, ladies," the porter says, breaking up our playful flirting. "I have breakfast for you."

After breakfast, Emery and I snuggle together by the

window, enjoying the rural scenery. The train's gentle rumble rocks us as we hold hands, listening to the clickety-clack of the wheels hitting the tracks.

"Emery, I never would have imagined you joining me on this excursion."

"Well, I did ask you years ago to be my girlfriend," she says with a chuckle.

"Yes, you most certainly did. How brave you were to give me that note that night."

"Come here, Emery," I say, drawing her into my arms. As we hold each other, we gaze out the window, watching the small towns flash by, the winding rivers, and the rolling hills as we near Atlanta.

Emery pulls away and stretches. "You calm me, Ingrid. I almost dozed off several times," she says, kissing my lips sweetly.

"You have that effect on me too, love. I feel safe with you, Emery."

"Safe is one thing you will always be with me," she says as she kisses me again. "I crave you, Ingrid."

Threading my fingers through her lovely hair, I gaze into her gray eyes—the same eyes that seduced me emotionally the night she picked me up at the airport.

"I believe we are in Atlanta now. We have three hours until we board the Panama Limited to Chicago, baby. What should we do, Emery?"

"We could take a taxi to The Fox Theatre if you'd like."

"That's a great idea. We can watch whatever is playing, return to the station, and catch the Panama Limited."

Exiting the taxi, I see 'The Unfaithful' with Ann Sheridan on the marquee, and I smile.

"I haven't seen this movie, Ingrid. Have you?"

"No, but I've wanted to. Ann is a very warm and charming lady. Very down to earth."

"Should I be jealous," Emery asks with a grin.

"Come on, silly, let's get our tickets." Settling into the coziness of the Theatre, Emery reaches for my hand. I lean in and whisper, "You never have to be jealous of anyone, love. You are my princess, Emery Wilde. Don't you ever forget that—or this moment."

She gazes at me and whispers, "Your princess?" I nod and wink at her. "I love that, Ingrid," she says.

As the theater goes dark before the film, I lean over, kiss Emery's sweet cheek, and whisper, "I love you."

CHAPTER ELEVEN: EMERY

Sitting in the dining car, after finishing our supper, I say "That was such a good meal, Ingrid. I can't eat like this all the way to San Francisco."

Ingrid sips on her coffee and grins. "A couple of pounds won't hurt you, love. I saw your toned legs and tummy the other morning."

Sipping on my coffee, I glance at her and grin. "Did you want me at that moment?"

Ingrid puts her coffee cup down, gazes into my eyes, and says, "Yes, I did, Emery. When you approached and sat next to me that morning before you left, the way you looked at me stirred something deep inside."

Leaning into her, I whisper, "You should have asked me to stay."

"I wanted to, Emery. But honey, I was still trying to come to terms with our age difference and the fact that I've practically watched you grow up."

"I understand, Ingrid," I say, with a wink and a smile. Would you like to return to our private compartment?"

Smiling at me, she whispers sweetly, "Yes. I'd love that."

Upon entering our private, cozy room, I pull Ingrid close, holding her tightly. "You're such a beautiful woman," I say as I reach up and gently remove the hair comb holding her hair up. Ingrid's long, dark locks fall onto her shoulders. Reaching for them, I thread my fingers through her soft hair, pull her to my lips, and kiss her tenderly.

Ingrid kisses me sweetly; her full lips are soft and tender. Her kisses bring a new, unfamiliar ache to my heart that I realize is becoming my new normal. Hugging her closely, I inhale her scent and enjoy her body against mine. I smile feeling complete contentment.

She guides me to the settee and pulls me close as we sit. "I feel twenty years younger with you, Emery. You make me incredibly happy."

"Good," I say with a grin.

As this magical train glides through the darkness, Ingrid and I discuss our upcoming destinations, our love for one another, and a million other things. Glancing at my watch, I say, "We should be in Chicago in approximately twelve hours."

"It's already ten p.m. love?"

"Yes, ma'am, it is, but I'm not sleepy. Are you?"

"No, I'm not either. Should I order a bottle of champagne like I did the first night we spent together?" she asks.

"Yes, I've eaten this time, I shouldn't get queasy."

"I'll take care of you again if you do," She says, then kisses my cheek.

"You doting on me that night made it all worthwhile. However, your sensual lingering scent drove me crazy as you sat beside me."

"Oh, Emery. Seriously?"

"You better believe it, woman." Ingrid grins at me as she shakes her head.

Standing, I say, "I'll go to the dining car and order the champagne. Would you like anything else, gorgeous?"

"Emery, you're so charming, baby. I can't think of anything else but you."

Returning with the champagne in an ice bucket and two glasses, I say, "I just waited for it so we wouldn't be disturbed."

Ingrid reaches out for me as I sit beside her and place the bucket on a small table. When I open the bottle, it starts foaming and gushing. Ingrid grabs a glass to catch the flowing suds and begins laughing. "My god, Emery, did you shake it up on the way back? I've never seen champagne come out so fast,"

"Yes, Ingrid, I shook the bottle up just for the hell of it," I say, laughing.

"It appears you must have!" she says, laughing uncontrollably. As it continues foaming, I turn the bottle up quickly and drink from it. "Emery!" she shouts with laughter.

The foaming finally stops, I grin at her, offering her the bottle. Ingrid meets my eyes, grabs the bottle, takes a big gulp and then places it back in the ice bucket. Laughing, I snatch the bottle and take another swig as Ingrid collapses into giggles.

"Next time I order, I'll say 'one bottle of champagne, hold the glasses.'" Ingrid roars with laughter as she grabs her glass of champagne and then me.

"Emery Wilde, you're too much."

Filling our glasses with what's left of the champagne, I gaze at her and ask, "What shall we toast to, Miss Mercer?" Ingrid is still laughing as she touches my cheek.

"You've brought my world to life, Emery Wilde. And I know that I am definitely in for a *WILD* ride with you, honey."

I wait for her toast, gazing at her with a grin and enjoying her happiness. "Let's toast to *'Our World's Aligning,'* Emery."

"That was in my love poem, wasn't it?"

"Yes, baby. It was."

"To 'Our World's Aligning,'" I say, then kiss her sweetly.

As the night lingers, I feel a warm relaxation from the champagne. "Should I ask the porter to convert our couch to a bed?"

Obviously feeling the same warmth, Ingrid leans to me as she whispers, "I think that's a splendid idea, Miss Wilde."

"So do I, Miss Mercer. I'll be right back."

After the porter leaves, Ingrid and I stretch out on the bed and immediately pull one another close." Do you have my sleep shirt?" I ask playfully.

Giggling, she says, "Yes, but I've worn it the past couple of nights because it smells like you, my love."

"Ingrid, that makes my heart smile."

Touching my face, she says, "Emery. I love the way you smell, baby."

"I don't know what to say." Ingrid rises, looks down at me, and smiles.

"Let's put our pajamas on, love. Okay?"

"Sure. I'll turn this lamp off so we only have the night lights. Is that okay?"

"Don't you want to see me, Emery?" she asks flirtatiously.

Gazing at her, I say, "Ingrid, I'm dying to see you, but I know we want to wait until Chicago." Turning off the lamp, Ingrid and I are bathed in the soft glow of the night light. "I want to take my time with you. I'd love to take you right now, but you're a lady, and I want to make love to you for the first time in a more proper place."

"Emery, my sweet love, yes, I want to wait too, baby."

After we dress for bed, we pull each other close under the covers. "You're my princess, Emery, so you deserve to be treated like one while I make love to you. Especially for the first time."

Pulling Ingrid closer, I whisper, "What did you say I am again?" I ask with a grin.

Touching my cheek, she whispers, "You're my princess, Emery Wilde. You will always be my sweet princess. I've adored you forever, baby."

"I love being your princess, Ingrid. You treat me like one."

"I always will, my love."

As Ingrid holds me in her arms, I close my eyes and inhale her aroma. "I love how you smell, baby. When you hugged me at the airport, your scent captivated me, and I couldn't let go. All I wanted to do was stand in that moment, feel you in my arms, and breathe you, Ingrid."

"Emery," She whispers. "I smelled you, too, and your aroma confused me."

"Why, Ingrid?"

"Because you smell like a woman now, not that sixteen-year-old girl with a crush on me. I still remember how you smelled back then, love."

Gazing up at her, I smile. She looks at me and says, "The scent you exude now is incredibly captivating and has an allure that intoxicates me."

Moving on top of Ingrid, I gaze into her eyes and recite my love note:

A fleeting glance, a moment's touch,
In every silent beat, I feel your presence.
When the world aligns, and your heart is free,
Find me, for though I am young, I'll wait for you patiently.

Ingrid gently touches my face and tenderly threads her fingers through my hair. We remain silent as the rhythmic rumble and clickety-clacks of the wheels on the tracks serenade us in this intimate moment. 'I love you, Ingrid,' I whisper.

As she smiles at me, I see her gazing at my lips. This tender moment feels fragile and pure, almost ethereal. Holding her in my arms, I smile and trace the outline of her lips with my fingertips. Our eyes meet, and I feel her soul singing to me, whispering a sweetheart's melody that only we can hear.

Kissing her tenderly, she parts her lips, and I feel the warmth of her tongue against mine. Her kisses are deliberately soft, and slow. My heart tumbles in response to each intimate touch. Pulling away, I gaze into her eyes and speak to her from my heart.

"Hold me, Emery," she whispers. I nod slowly, pulling her into my arms, and love her tenderly as she lies against my body.

"Goodnight, Ingrid. I love you."

She sighs, snuggles closer to me, and whispers, "Goodnight, my princess."

I close my eyes and I replay her beautiful words over-and-over in my heart and mind, 'Goodnight, my princess.' I smile as we hold each other intimately, surrendering to midnight's embrace.

CHAPTER TWELVE: INGRID

Sitting beside Emery, we watch the snow blow past us in the fading light as we near Chicago. "Look at this beautiful snow that's welcoming us, Emery," I say excitedly, then grab her hands. They immediately interlock as we watch the snowflakes gather and dance for us.

"It's like a magical dream, Ingrid. This snow makes me feel like a kid again. I've experienced it so few times; I'm in awe." I glance at Emery, and see her eyes twinkling as she watches the snowfall whisk past us and the tall buildings greet us. She kisses my hand, then looks at me with a smile.

We hear the train conductor make an announcement throughout the cars:

"Ladies and gentlemen, this is your conductor. We are now approaching Chicago and will soon arrive at Union Station. Please check that you have all your belongings as we prepare to disembark. Thank you for traveling with us on the Panama Limited. We wish you a pleasant stay in Chicago."

. . .

The porter graciously transferred our luggage from the baggage claim to the station's taxi stand. The taxi driver loaded our luggage, and now Emery and I are in the back of the taxi on our way to the hotel.

"Ma'am, did you say, "The Avalon Grande?" asks the taxi driver.

"Yes, please," I reply, squeezing Emery's hand. She leans over and kisses my cheek. Smiling at her, I wink and say, "We are in Chicago, my princess."

Emery's whole face lights up, and I see her happiness and love for me. We sit huddled together, watching the snow cascade, its beauty illuminated by the glow of the street lamps. "This beautiful snow is following us," Emery softly whispers against my loose hair.

"Yes, it seems to be. Perhaps you have charmed it as you have me, Miss Wilde." She giggles against me, warming my heart.

Pulling up to the hotel, we are met by a bellhop who kindly unloads our luggage and patiently waits for us to check-in. I stand next to Emery, as she checks us in at the front desk as planned. The last thing either of us wants on this romantic getaway is for me to be recognized or the two of us to be discovered.

Walking into our grand suite, I stand and watch Emery as the bellhop unloads our luggage, thoughtfully placing it by the huge wardrobe. "Thank you," Emery says, offering him his gratuity, as he leaves.

As I stand near the massive window, I gaze out at the city lights and watch the snow continue to fall softly. I close my eyes and I wait to feel her arms around me. Smiling, I smell her as she wraps her arms around my waist from behind. I take a deep breath, inhaling her. Then I open my eyes and gaze back out at the tumbling snow.

"Should I order champagne?" she whispers in my ear.

Turning toward her, I cup her cheek, and touch her lips with mine. I wrap my arms around her neck and pull her close.

Pulling away, I gaze into her eyes. "Yes, please, my love." She releases me gently and turns to walk toward the phone. I take her hand, and she glances back at me.

"Darling, order some bread, as well; you haven't eaten in a while."

She winks at me and grins. "I will, baby." Emery walks back to me and says, "Go take a bath if you'd like, Ingrid. I'll wait on room service and then bathe after you."

Walking to her, I ask, "You don't mind?"

"No, baby, go ahead. Besides, it will give me more time to give the champagne bottle a good shake," she says mischievously. Laughing, I walk by her, and give her a playful spank on the ass, then keep my hand there for a moment as I kiss her cheek.

Continuing my walk to the bathroom, Emery playfully shouts, "Tease!" Laughing loudly, I shake my head and enter the bathroom, giggling like a silly schoolgirl. After undressing, I step into the warm tub, sinking gently into the bubbles. I can't help but long for Emery to be in the tub with me.

Listening, I hear room service come and go. Then a soft knock makes me grin. "Yes?"

"Would you like some champagne, Ingrid?" She asks sweetly

"Yes, Emery. Please come in." The door opens slowly, and my eyes merge Emery's. This is the moment we've yearned for, and we both know it immediately.

"May I join you, Ingrid?"

"Emery, there's nothing I'd love more."

She walks in and sets the champagne bucket on the edge of the tub, and turns to walk out. "I'll be right back," she says sweetly.

Entering the room once again, I see her smiling with two

candles in her hands. She winks at me as she lights them. I admire her loveliness and smile at her romantic heart. Emery starts to undress while I lean back and gaze at her.

I'm longing to see her perfect breasts and body again—I only got a peek at her few days ago. Emery holds my gaze as she undresses slowly. She removes her last garment, her panties, stands nude before me, and allows me to look at her beautiful body in the soft candlelight. "You're so lovely, Emery. Please come to me, my princess."

As she moves toward me, I see her full bosoms, and I almost gasp. Sitting up, I reach for her hand. She steps into the warm bubble water with me, gazing down at me. "You are the most gorgeous woman I've ever known, Emery Wilde. Thank you for allowing me to love you."

Lowering her body into the tub, with a smile she says, "I've wanted you for so long, Ingrid. I never thought the love note I wrote to you years ago would lead to this. But I know my love for you was very pure, just as it is now."

"Yes, Emery, our love is so pure. You're almost too perfect for me to touch. Does that sound silly?"

"No, it doesn't, Ingrid. I understand. I'm a bit nervous, baby," she says as she pulls her knees up to her body.

"It's just me, darling, but I understand. I'm nervous too. I want this night to be perfect, especially for you—I want to show you how much I love you."

Opening the champagne, she glances at me and whispers, "It will be perfect. It already is."

Emery pops the top on the champagne, giggling. "I forgot to shake it." We both laugh as she pours the bubbly into our glasses and hands one of them to me.

Touching our glasses together, she whispers, *"To the world aligning for us, Ingrid."*

With tears pooling in my eyes, I gaze at the young woman who penned those words for me years ago. I whisper,

"Emery, those beautiful words were scored into my heart many moons ago."

She smiles sweetly at me, sips her champagne, and gazes out the window. "The snow is falling heavier. It's so beautiful and mystical."

Emery lies back across from me, sipping her champagne as we gaze at each other, enjoying this intimate moment. "It's so quiet, especially after the train tracks rumbling and clacking beneath us all day and night."

"Yes, it's intimately quiet."

"Ingrid, I drifted off into a glorious slumber last night as I cradled you in my arms. I remember surrendering to the embrace of the Divine and the safety of your love."

"Emery, you have the heart and soul of a poet. You're such a deep and complex woman. You always have been."

She looks at me oddly. "Yes, Emery, even when you were young, I could see how special and mysterious you were. Now, you've grown into an incredible woman with even more depth. You have many deep layers that I wish to explore. It will take me years to truly understand you."

"I'll always be open with you, Ingrid. One thing you'll never have to wonder about is my love for you. No matter how complex or deep you think I am, my heart will always be open to you."

Smiling, I break off some bread, and ask Emery to come closer. She moves between my legs onto her side. Holding her close, I feed her a piece. "Thank you, Ingrid. I love how you nurture me."

Holding the bread to her, I whisper, "You're my princess. I'll always nurture you."

"I love being in your arms against your breasts like this." she says, pulling away slightly, gazing into my eyes, and tucking a lock of hair behind my ear. "I am going to love you all night long, Ingrid Mercer. You are mine, and I'm going to shower you with this immense love I've held for you all these years."

"Why don't we stop with the champagne for now. I want to have a clear heart and lucid mind, as I take you for the first time," I whisper, as I kiss her cheek sweetly.

Emery nods and offers me a piece of bread. After I swallow, I ask, "Do you want to stay here or go to the bedroom, Emery?"

"I'm loving this, Ingrid."

Hugging her, I say, "Me too. I could stay in this warm bath with you for hours."

CHAPTER THIRTEEN: EMERY

After Ingrid opens a soap bar, she begins lathering it onto a sea sponge. Smiling at her, she starts gently bathing me. Turning away from her, she washes my back, tenderly whispering, "You're so lovely." My heart and soul feel as though they might collapse under her seductive touch.

"Ingrid," I whisper.

"Does this feel good, Emery?"

All I can do is moan and submit to her love. "Yes," I whisper. Turning back and facing her, I see her eyes have grown curious and provocative. Seeing her desire for me, I take the sponge from her and bathe her with the same tenderness.

Ingrid closes her eyes, sighing, and then whispering, "Oh, Emery." Gazing at her, I long to see her beautiful body hidden beneath the suds. Holding her in my arms, I continue bathing her tenderly.

Bravely, I reach for her sex and begin bathing it with the sea sponge. Opening her eyes, she meets my gaze. She looks at my lips, moves closer to them, and tenderly bites the lower one as I continue bathing her feminine essence.

Letting the sea sponge float away, I take her sanctuary in my hand. Feeling her sexually in the warm water causes me to go weak. "Ingrid, the effect you're having on me is almost too much."

"Come here, Emery, she says softly." Pulling me closer, she whispers, "There's no rush, my love." As she holds me I feel a little embarrassed that I couldn't go on.

Lying against her breasts, I whisper, "Now that I have you, I'm gripped with fear, Ingrid. I'm sorry, I hate this."

"My sweet Emery, it's understandable." She looks into my eyes, smiles, and tenderly kisses my lips. "Why don't we dry off and move to the bedroom?"

Smiling, I say, "I think that would help. You've cast a spell on me amidst the falling snow and the warmth of this tub. I can't seem to pull myself away."

Hugging me, she says, "Oh, Emery, you'll find that sexy confidence soon enough. Don't you worry. As I said, we have all night."

Gazing into her eyes, I ask, "Ingrid, will you step out of the tub and let me look at your gorgeous body as you dry off?"

She grins at me as she rises. Almost falling against the back of the tub, I see my crush from years ago standing before me. "My god, you're gorgeous," I say breathlessly.

Ingrid's body is even more beautiful than I could have imagined. I finally see her full erotic bosoms—the ones I touched that night on the beach. As she steps out of the tub, I rest my crossed arms on the tub's edge watching her. She turns her back to me, letting me take in her lovely curves and slopes and the roundness of her ass. It's firm and just waiting to be touched.

She turns around toward me, and our hungry eyes meet. I gaze at her feminine mound, aching to taste and explore it.

"My god, your breasts are beautiful, Ingrid." Her bosoms

are full and firm, exuding power as her nipples stand erect, begging to be loved.

Waves of overpowering desire mixed with fearful anxiety crash over me as I watch Ingrid drying off her wet body.

I sit in the water, watching my woman as she continues drying off. She's waiting patiently for me. Feeling my erotic core burn and my anxiety wane, I stand, step out of the tub, and approach her.

Ingrid grins as she takes a fresh towel and begins drying me. Her grin widens; she knows I have found my confidence. I grin back at her. "Let's go to bed, baby," I say.

Taking her hand, we walk into the bedroom and over to the massive windows. "The snow is still falling for us, Ingrid," I say as we stand nude, watching the snow, waiting for this intimate and magical moment to unfold.

Drawing her closer, I gaze into her exotic green eyes and kiss her lips tenderly. "Stay here; I'll turn down the bed covers for us." She touches my face and winks at me.

Ingrid is watching the snow as I prepare our bed. I can't help but smile and steal glances at her as I prepare the bed. Walking back to her, I wrap my arms around her from behind, and pull her erotic body against mine, as I whisper in her ear, "May I take you to bed now?" I feel her nod. Taking her hand, I lead her to the bed.

Under the covers, I pull her close to me and feel her womanness against mine. "You feel incredible, Ingrid."

Ingrid moves on top of me, lifts her hand, removing her hair comb and allowing her dark hair to fall. Watching this sends intense vibrations throughout my extremities and an aching pulsing in my sexual center. She gathers her hair to one side and gazes at me. Reaching out, I thread my fingers through her hair and draw her closer to my lips.

Suddenly, my body awakens, burning with intense heat for this woman. Leaving one hand entangled in her dark hair, the other reaches for that perfect round ass I saw just moments ago.

Gripping her tighter, my erotic love for her intensifies. Our kisses grow hungry as I feel our familiar and undeniable chemistry. Yes, there is the erotic lust I've felt for her since she walked into my arms at the airport.

Ingrid feels it, too; her passion for me is apparent. I open my lips for her—our tongues collide and twirl in unison. Breaking our kiss, Ingrid looks into my eyes as she whispers, "I love you, Emery." Smiling at her, I touch her face and bring her lips back to mine. Our tongues revel as they meet again.

Rising slowly, Ingrid moves onto my lap. I hold her tightly and continue passionately loving her mouth with intense fervor. Pulling away reluctantly, I gaze at her full bosoms and grin as I take them in my hands. I begin to brush my thumbs across her nipples just as I did that night on the beach.

Gazing into her eyes, I feel her nipples becoming erect—I roll them between my fingers and thumbs. Ingrid places her hands on top of mine and begins to moan. Tugging at them gently, I watch as her gaze is fixed on me. She whispers, "Yes, baby."

"Like this?" I ask as I tug them harder. Ingrid nods as she looks into my eyes hungrily, continuing to hold her hands against mine. I remember what Ingrid said about how she loves my playful, wicked side. I grin as I feel it emerge.

Releasing her breasts, I wrap my arms around this gorgeous vixen and grasp her with lustful rawness. Ingrid meets my passion as she threads her hands through my hair, holding my face against hers. Her seductive body, sitting on top of me, is sending spikes of electricity through every nerve ending in my body.

My carnal lust escalates. Grabbing Ingrid, I pull her off of me in one swift movement and roll on top of her, pushing my erotic zone against her. I can barely breathe with her mouth on mine, and the panting sounds I'm making with each thrust against her. Pushing one leg between hers, I feel her wetness and begin to move against it. Ingrid grabs my ass, pulling me closer, needing more. She begins to push against me, riding me as she moans, holding my mouth and tongue hostage.

I gently grip one of her bosoms with my right hand and brush against the nipple with my thumb again. It peaks instantly. Tugging it, I increase my rhythm against her as my moans and pants increase. Suddenly, Ingrid pulls away to gaze at me and simply moans, "Emery."

Continuing to move against her, I meet her eyes and see her intense desire to be taken. Moving to her breasts, I cup them in my hands and begin to swirl my tongue over each one, sucking them tenderly and flicking my tongue against her peaks.

Ingrid keeps her fingers entangled in a few locks of my hair as she watches me love her.

Moving down to her tummy, I begin loving it with long, slow licks. I look up at her and wink, then start slowly licking from below her belly button all the way to those perfect peaks of hers. Over and over, I continue kissing her belly and nipples, flicking each nipple when I reach it.

As I reach her nipple, she grasps my hair tightly as she says, "I was right, you are very wicked, Miss Wilde."

"Too wicked for you, Miss Mercer?" I ask with a grin.

"Oh no, honey. Your wickedness is part of your charm." I laugh, then bite her tummy, and she moans. "I'm enjoying the hell out of you," she says with a chuckle.

I begin to lick her just above her feminine mound as I gaze at her. She gives me an erotic grin—wanting me on her clit, but she's appreciating my willingness to take her slowly and seductively. Kissing her sweet mound, I move back towards her face and grin.

Looking at me, perplexed, I lie on my back, looking at her then giving her a wink. Ingrid giggles, climbs on top of me, straddles me. She sits with her wetness against mine, and we hold hands and smile at each other. I gaze up at her, and she begins moving against me, pushing her wetness against mine. Holding her hips, I begin upward movements as we find our rhythm. Touching her clit with my thumb, she stops and gasps.

Gazing up at her, I say, "I want your swollen sweet clit in my mouth, Miss Mercer." She gives me an almost unbelievable look as I pull her towards my mouth. She reaches me and then looks down at me in disbelief. "Come on, baby. Let me taste your sweet fruit. I've wanted to taste you for years." I say seductively.

Moving onto my mouth, I smell her and am overcome by another wave of wicked lust. I reach and grab her ass, pulling her against my mouth. She moans, "Emery," and I begin to move my tongue in uniform movements back and forth across her clit. Ingrid reaches for the headboard and finds her rhythm.

As Ingrid rocks against my mouth, moaning and whispering my name, she continues gripping the headboard. Grabbing her ass harder, I can't help but dig my short nails into her ass as my body craves her.

Ingrid tastes and smells, unlike any other woman I've known. Her essence is exotic. Made up of a subtle musk with a hint of sweetness that is utterly captivating and erotic. I feel Ingrid reaching close to climax as she continues rocking her body against my mouth. Glancing up, I catch a glimpse of her as she grasps the bed, and I feel seduced all over again.

"Emery, this feels amazing." She's so close. I feel her on my tongue and know she is almost there. Glancing at her hands on the headboard again awakens something profound within me—something carnal and animalistic. Grasping her bosoms, she lets out an intense moan as I begin to tug at her nipples. I feel her letting go and she releases herself to me. Slowly, she says, "Emery, baby. I'm coming."

She isn't releasing the headboard, and my lust continues to burn as I keep her in my mouth, continuing to love her clit with fierceness. Again, she says, "I'm coming, Emery." I feel her riding this intense orgasm. As she releases the headboard, she looks down at me and touches my face. "Oh, god, Emery."

She moves off of me slowly, unaware that I'm not done with her. Pushing her gently onto the bed, I kiss her passionately. Ingrid reaches around my neck, and I feel her legs open for me. I suppose she knows me better than I realized. Lowering my body a bit, I reach for her clit and begin moving my fingers firmly and unyielding in circular motions as I gaze at her.

Looking into her eyes, I softly say, "Your taste intoxicates me." Then I lean in closer and whisper in her ear. "I've craved your intimate essence for years, Ingrid."

Pulling back gently to watch her, I gaze into those exotic green eyes and watch her become vulnerable to my touch. "Do I taste how you expected me to, love?" She whispers onto my lips.

Pressing firmer against her clit I whisper back, "Exactly how I've fantasized, baby."

Ingrid is watching my face, and I see her giving into me again, "Emery, honey." With eyes wide open, she orgasms, allowing me to watch her tumble and fall.

"Yes, Ingrid. Come for me, baby." She comes again, staring into my eyes. After her orgasm, I go inside and begin giving short, sharp pushes into her core. Ingrid is shaking her head.

"Emery, what in the hell are you doing to me?"

Taking one of her nipples in my mouth, I begin to suck it and flick it with my tongue as my fingers fuck her sexual tunnel with wicked intensity. Watching her, I continue gaining momentum. "I thought you loved my wickedness," I say as I increase my tempo, hitting her sexual core with more intensity.

"I do, but I had no idea you were this wicked."

"Well, maybe you should have inquired before you allowed me to bed you, Miss Mercer."

"Damn you, Emery Wilde," She says with a grin, enjoying every bit of thrust she's receiving.

Rising to my knees, I gaze down at her, and I continue fucking her intensely. "Emery, please don't stop, baby. You're amazing."

"I'll fuck you all night." Looking into her exotic eyes, I confess, "I've wanted to fuck you for years, so I have a lot of pent-up desire that needs to be released."

"That's obvious. You're incredible, Emery."

Tugging one of her nipples, I continue hitting her sacred core. "Come for me again, baby."

Closing her eyes, Ingrid surrenders completely to me. "Yes, Emery. Don't stop fucking me. I'll come for you again, baby." With that, she releases a crying moan as I gaze at her. I think to myself what a gorgeous woman she is as she lets go. Free falling into an uncontrollable climax. Opening her eyes to greet mine, I smile, keeping the same tempo, letting her continue to ride the rest of this orgasm.

When she's finished, she reaches her arms out for me and whispers, "Hold me, Emery."

Pulling out slowly, I lie against her, putting my arms underneath her, offering her my entire body. She takes a deep breath and sighs. "I'm so in love with you, Emery."

Smiling, I continue holding her in my arms. "I'm in love with you, Ingrid. I always have been."

CHAPTER FOURTEEN: INGRID

Gently moving off of me, she sits up, gazing out the bedroom window and says, "Our snowflakes are still falling."

As I sit beside her, she draws me close. "Look, Ingrid, it's even heavier now."

Reaching my arms around Emery, I pull her close and kiss her shoulder. "Yes, it is, baby." I love that the snow is still falling for us.

"Ingrid, It feels as though you and I are inside a massive SnowGlobe filled with billions of snowflakes. And they are dancing and celebrating our love for one another."

"Emery, that's beautiful. You are my princess, so you should be kept safe inside this SnowGlobe with me forever," I say, then kiss her soft shoulder again. Lying against her, I wait, letting her continue gazing out the glass window of our lovely snow globe. The falling snow makes me feel her youth, and instead of feeling somber, I smile, overwhelmed by my love for her. As I gaze out the window beside her, I suddenly hear her love note whispering: *'Find Me.'*

Tears pool in my eyes as I begin to wonder if her sweet

love note is a living organism—one she cultivated with words from her heart and that I nourished by cherishing it over it all these years. Our love has flourished, and will only continue to thrive. Closing my eyes, I realize that's what has happened. Yes, Emery was always meant to be mine.

Emery turns away from the falling snow and looks into my eyes. Resting my chin on her shoulder, I whisper, "That was incredible, Emery. I've never felt such a passionate yet tender force before. You're incredibly strong and loving. As I said before, I have no intentions of ever taming you."

"You bring this out in me, Ingrid. You make me incredibly raw and untamable."

Giggling, I say, "Perhaps, but I believe this is your natural state, my lovely, wild one."

Laughing, Emery says, "You think so?"

Nodding, I grin at her with a wink.

"Are you hungry, Ingrid?"

Whispering "yes" in her ear, I gently push her onto the bed with my body and gaze down at her. "I'm famished for you, my princess." Then I ask, "Is there a specific place I might feed on that will cure my hunger?"

Emery smiles at me, then lovingly threads her fingers through my hair. "You may feast on any part of my body you wish."

"That's exactly what I am going to do, Miss Wilde," I say with a grin. Gazing at Emery, I feel an overwhelming love for her. My heart whispers, *'Love her tenderly,'* but my hungry body boldly says, *'NO! Devour her.'*

Easing against her warm body, I put my arms around her, drawing her close, and then kissing her sweet lips tenderly. Gazing into her eyes, my heart wins. I will have years to take her forcefully, but only once to take her for the first time.

As I continue to kiss her slowly and tenderly, I feel her relaxing beneath me. She whispers, "Yes, Ingrid." How could I take her any other way at this moment? Gazing back into her eyes, I feel her love so intensely—it makes me want to weep. Emery truly has loved me all these years, much more profoundly than I could have imagined.

"I love you, Emery. You are so pure and full of kindness, my love." Lying on top of her, I take her hands in mine and move them above her head. Our fingers interlock, and I continue kissing her softly. Holding her arms down, I move to her neck, kissing it with the same tenderness, and then bite it gently. Emery lets out a soft moan.

I remember how she stood before me while dressing in my hotel room, and I think about her perfect nipples and how desperately I want them in my mouth now.

Moving down, I take her full bosoms in my hands as I gaze at her. Emery smiles sweetly, then pushes her fingers through my hair while watching me. I can't help but admire her beauty. With her eyes still fixed on me, I swipe my thumbs across her perfect nipples and watch them rise for me.

"You're mine," I whisper to her. I take one of her nipples in my mouth, closing my eyes as I suck slowly. My god, she feels so good in my mouth. Cupping her breast, I tenderly suck on each one, loving the same bosoms I've thought about non-stop since that morning in my hotel room. Emery begins moving her body, needing more from me.

Moving back to her face, I gaze at her and whisper, "Roll over, princess."

Without hesitation, she turns to her tummy. As I look down at her, I can't help but take in her sensual body, "Baby, you are incredible. Your body is gorgeous."

"Thank you," she whispers softly.

Rising up, I stretch my entire body out, then slowly lower it onto hers. Emery breathlessly whispers, "Oh god, Ingrid."

"Yes, my love?"

"You feel so delicious, Ingrid. My body aches for you." Rising up again, I begin licking her shoulders—long, slow licks from one shoulder to the other, taking my time as I love my beautiful woman. I move down and start kissing her back, then I lick her from her ass to her shoulder, making one long trail of wetness.

As I move to her ass, I cup it in my hands and begin to give it playful bites; Emery moans, giggles, and whimpers all at once. "Ingrid. You're incredible."

Smiling, I continue loving her. Looking at her ass, I long to taste it, so I lower my tongue between her cheeks and lick her from one end to the other. Slow, intentional licks, letting her know that I intend on loving every inch of her, and nothing is off limits.

Rising again, I move between her legs and reach to touch her. She is soaked, causing my erotic desire to burn more passionately. I close my eyes, still intent to take her tenderly. Emery opens her legs, knowing what I crave. I move back to her ass, kiss it, and then find her soaked gateway. Entering her slowly, I keep my lips on her ass, and my eyes on her sweet face.

Emery lifts her hips, allowing me to enter her deeper. I push in tenderly, and she lets out a soft moan. Holding my fingers inside her, I continue to lick her ass. Emery begins to push her body against my fingers, begging me to take her. I start giving her slow, tender thrusts, and we find a tender rhythm.

I rest my head on her ass, and we continue this gentle rhythmic dance. I've never been this lovingly tender with anyone, but Emery isn't just anyone. She is indeed my princess, full of goodness—the one who has loved me forever.

"Do you like this, love?" I ask.

"Yes, baby. You're so gentle with me, Ingrid. You have me

hypnotized and under your spell again." My heart feels as though it might explode as I watch her moving against my fingers. After a moment, I pull out gently and lay my body against hers once again. "Turn over, love," I ask her.

I pull her close, we lie facing each other, our eyes locked in a shared gaze I thread my fingers through her hair as I pull her to my lips and open my mouth for her. Emery wraps her arms around me and pulls me tight. Our kisses ignite, burning hotter every moment. I feel her lust and her need to be taken harder, as I push my tongue against hers.

With one arm under her neck, I move the other one to her hip and pull her against me and I begin moving my sex against hers. Emery moans, grabs my ass and presses herself into me.

As I reach between her legs, I find her flooded gateway once again. Then I gather her warm fluid, bring it back to her clit, and touch it softly. Emery whimpers quietly. As I move my fingers against her clit in soft, tender circles, she continues whimpering. I move to her ear and whisper, "Does this feel good, princess?"

"Yes, Ingrid. You know it does." Smiling, I love her tenderly, not allowing myself to grow forceful with her. "I love you," she whispers.

Kissing her cheek tenderly, I whisper back, "I love you, Emery."

Looking into her eyes, I say softly, "I want you in my mouth." Our eyes lock, and she nods with a smile.

As I lie back, Emery moves on top of me and pushes herself into my mouth. I immediately inhale and smell her sweetness. Watching her with her hands on the headboard, I move my hands to her breasts and cup them, tenderly brushing my thumbs over her nipples. My body feels like a blazing fire, with intense heat coursing through every nerve ending.

Emery looks down at me, and our eyes meet. She begins slowly moving against my tongue. I plunge deep inside, needing to feed on her sweetness, then I swallow her liquid. With my tongue on her swollen clit, I begin loving it tenderly. As she moves gently against my mouth, she finds a tender rhythm, and I know that she is enjoying every moment.

Holding her gaze, I wink at her; she winks back as she rides me slowly, and gives me soft, sweet whimpers. I feel her clit harden and know she's close—my tongue pushes harder. She gasps breathlessly saying, "Oh, yes, Ingrid."

She grips the headboard tightly, and pushes down against my tongue, as she holds my gaze. As she increases her rhythm, I meet her tempo and feel her growing weak. I grab her body, hold her firmly. I want her to feel my strength, so she knows she can let go, knowing I'll catch her when she tumbles. As she grabs my arms, and I hold her upright, Emery lets go, "Ingrid, I love you," she cries out softly.

With our eyes and bodies connected, I watch the woman I love fall tenderly into my soul. She's weeping but continues to ride me, allowing me to hold her. Emery continues gazing at me and whispers, "I'm coming, Ingrid." Her eyes fill with tears, but they remain locked on mine as she falls once again for me, and then closes her pretty eyes.

Emery moves to my hips, straddling me. I sit up, grab her, and pull her against me with all of my strength. "It's okay, my sweet Emery. I'm here and love you just as you've wanted me to all these years. I'll love you forever, Emery."

With her arms around my neck, she kisses my cheek and then melts against my body. Over the last several days Emery has revealed her strength to me, but this is the first time I've seen her so vulnerable. It's beautiful, stirring something in me that I haven't felt before. Her vulnerability uncovers a side of myself I hadn't fully realized—a deep protectiveness and intense desire to nurture her.

Holding her tightly, I gaze out the window, watching the snow continue to fall in celebration of our love. Emery is right; it feels like we're a single entity inside this immense SnowGlobe. I have no desire to leave this magical place. This moment is pure and loving, much like the tender note she penned for me moons ago when she planted the seeds of our love.

She pulls away, looks at me, and smiles. Touching her cheeks, I look into her eyes and see her soul—it's even more beautiful than I realized. Gently running my fingers through her soft hair, I look into her eyes and say, "Emery Wilde, you belong to me now, and I'll never let you go. Do you understand?" I ask with a serious heart.

Emery searches my eyes and sees the love I have for her. She nods and whispers, 'Yes, I understand I belong to you, Ingrid." Gazing at me, she threads her fingers through my hair and adds, "Do you understand that you belong to me, Ingrid Mercer, and that you always have?"

With tearful eyes, I whisper, "Yes, Emery, I understand I've always belonged to you. Your love note is proof of that, my love."

CHAPTER FIFTEEN: EMERY

Straddling Ingrid as she holds me, I feel the depth of her incredible love for me. "I love being in your arms, Ingrid."

She pulls me closer and she whispers, "Something profound happened to me while making love to you. I can't fully explain it, but I suddenly feel incredibly protective of your heart and soul, Emery. I'll never hurt or betray you, love."

Searching her face, I see an expression I've never seen before. "Ingrid, you look different. Are you okay?"

"I've never been more okay in my life, Emery." she replies with the same serious look. "Everything has become incredibly real and serious for me, and I understand what loving you has done to me."

Touching her face, I gaze at her, sensing the depths of her feelings for me. "I feel it, Ingrid."

"Good. Emery. Everything will be as it was before—I cherish our playful flirting and everything else. But, I want you to know that I'm committed to you and always will be. This is very serious to me."

Touching her face, I say, "Yes, I know, darling. It overwhelms me, but it also brings me immense joy. I've never seen this side of you before, Ingrid."

She gazes at me with the same intensity. "I didn't know I had this in me until now. It might take me some time to process, but I understand how this love for you has changed me, Emery."

"Is that a good thing, Ingrid?"

Touching my face, she smiles sweetly and says, "Yes, Emery. It is a very good thing, my love."

"That makes me happy." I pull Ingrid close to me and inhale her scent. "You were incredibly tender with me, baby, and my orgasms were incredible."

"That's how I wanted it the first time I made love to you, Emery. I couldn't have taken you any other way."

"It was beautiful, Ingrid," I whisper.

"That's how it should have been, love. And you taste amazing, Miss Wilde," she says with a giggle. Ingrid pulls me to her lips and kisses me sweetly. "I'm going to order room service. I need to feed you. Do you have any requests?" she asks.

Hugging her, I say, "Surprise me, I'll eat anything."

Ingrid spanks my leg and laughs, "Okay baby, let me up, and I'll order some food."

Whispering in her ear, I say, "Don't order dessert. I'll feed that to you later."

Ingrid grabs me tightly, whisking me off of her and onto my back, her body pressing against mine. With a playful laugh, she asks, "And what will I be having for dessert, Miss Wilde?"

Laughing, I say, "You must wait and see, Miss Mercer."

Ingrid gazes into my eyes, and I can see her love. The profound moment we shared earlier moved me deeply, though it seems to have unsettled her. I understand her feelings because I, too, am completely committed to this woman.

Standing by the couch, I pause, captivated as Ingrid glides across the room. She's wearing a floor-length midnight blue evening gown that perfectly accentuates her curves. Her dark hair is elegantly pinned up with a rhinestone comb, revealing her graceful neck. "Ingrid, you take my breath away in this velvet gown. It's absolutely stunning on you. Are you really mine?"

Ingrid walks gracefully toward me, her smile radiant as she gently touches my cheek. "Emery Wilde, yes, my love, I'm all yours. And I'm hopelessly in love with you."

My heart races, a thrilling jolt running through my body as I gaze at my beautiful forty-six-year-old lover. "You're breathtaking," I whisper, overwhelmed by the sight of her.

"Thank you, Miss Wilde. And you, my love, are breathtaking in this black tailored suit. Your sexy curves fit these slacks divinely. The suit perfectly compliments your energy and charisma, while the crisp white blouse highlights your honey-colored hair. You are an absolute beauty, Emery," she says, as she kisses my lips sweetly.

"Thank you, Ingrid."

"You're welcome. Will you sit on the sofa for a moment? I'll be right back."

Sitting on the sofa, fussing with my sleeves, I notice Ingrid walking toward me with a small box. She sits beside me and smiles. Smiling back, I ask, "What's this, baby?"

"A gift for you. The first of so many more to come, Emery. Please open it."

Gazing at Ingrid nearly takes my breath away. "Tonight,

you're making me incredibly nervous," I say, touching her cheek and looking into her exotic green eyes. As I open the small box, I see an elegant rhinestone bracelet.

Looking at this beautiful bracelet, I can't help but know that I am truly her woman and lover. "This is incredibly beautiful, Ingrid. I don't know what to say."

"You don't have to say anything. Let me put it on you, Emery." As Ingrid fastens around my wrist, I can't help but smile, my heart overflowing with love for her. When she clasps the bracelet, she lifts her eyes to meet mine. "You belong to me, Emery."

Touching her cheek, I nod and whisper, "Yes, I do." Glancing at the bracelet, I ask, "It's beautiful, Ingrid. When did you buy it? I've been with you the whole time."

"I bought it the morning after our first kiss."

"You bought it that long ago? How did you know?"

"That morning as I bared my soul to Lillian about how much I love you and my intentions, I felt an instinctive desire to buy you something meaningful. I stopped by a nearby jewelry store and saw this in the display case; it made me think of you."

"I love it, Ingrid, especially knowing you bought it after our first kiss. You're a romantic fool just like me."

"With you, I am."

"Ingrid, our trip has been like a mystical dream. Last night, making love to you was unbelievable. I loved your gentleness; my orgasms were so tender yet profound."

"I felt that Emery, and I saw it on your face when I looked up at you. Seeing you fall so tenderly brought out such a deep seriousness in me."

"That moment will stay with me forever, Ingrid. I've never seen you like that before. I love that side of you. Your protectiveness is incredibly alluring."

She smiles at me and says, "It's not just about your age, Emery. It's because I'm so in love with you. I want to keep you close to my heart at all times."

"Ingrid, you're going to make me cry and mess up the makeup that I applied, just for you," I tell her.

"Well, don't do that, love," she laughs. "Or we might end up back in that bed we left just over an hour ago."

"I could crawl right back into that bed and make love all night and tomorrow just as we've done all day, Ingrid."

Ingrid rises, offering me her hand as she laughs. "I'll take you up on that when we return from dinner and the show."

Taking her hand, I stand, smile into her eyes, and say, "You've got a date, Miss Mercer."

"Let's be off; the taxi will be here soon. This evening will be wonderful, just like every moment with you."

In the taxi, Ingrid and I huddle together, and watch the snow fall. "I'm excited to see *Carousel*, Ingrid. When you plan a date, you really go all out, don't you?" I say with a grin and a wink.

"Nothing is too grand for you, Emery. And, yes, I'm looking forward to seeing it as well. One day, I'll take you to Broadway to see all the shows, princess."

"Ingrid, I'm perfectly happy riding the beach with you in my Willys."

She laughs and says, "I know you are, and I love being out there with you. Next time we go to that secluded cove, we'll need more blankets," she says with a wink.

"Do you think next time I take you to that cove and build a nice hot fire, I'll be able to seduce you, Miss Mercer?" I whisper in her ear.

"You most definitely will. You practically seduced me that first night by the fire." Glancing back at me, she whispers, "You had me within a breath of an orgasm that night."

After checking to make sure the taxi driver isn't listening, I rest my chin on her shoulder and whisper, "I should have just taken you."

Grinning at me, she softly says, "You could have. I was completely helpless."

"Well, I'll compensate for that when we return to the hotel tonight. Let me ask you this, and be honest: what would you have done if I had just taken you?"

"Dammit, Emery. Do you have any idea what you're doing to me right now?"

"Yes, I do, but you didn't answer my question."

Ingrid looks at me, astonished, and shakes her head. "Answer me, Ingrid."

Turning to face me, she gazes intently and whispers, "You need to be taught a lesson, young lady."

"And who will my teacher be?" I ask with a chuckle.

The taxi driver interrupts our sexual flirting, "Here we are, folks. This is your stop."

Stepping out of the taxi, I stand and turn, and look down to meet my beautiful lover's eyes. "May I help you, Miss Mercer?" I ask, offering her my hand. She takes it gracefully as she steps out, her touch sending a familiar warmth through me.

Taking my hand, she stands, walks towards me, and takes my arm as I escort her to the restaurant. Just before I open the door, she says, "Please step over here, Emery." Pulling me close under the falling snow, she brings her face within inches of mine and whispers, "I'll answer your question, Emery." I nod, my grin widening. "I would have done anything you asked of me in that secluded cove."

Holding her close, I whisper, "I love that answer. Watching how I affected you that night is a moment I'll never forget."

She looks at me and smiles, "Let's have dinner, baby. Okay?"

Ingrid laughs, and I open the door for my lovely woman, holding her hand as we step inside. She looks at me and winks. "By the way, you look amazing; you're a damn knock-out, Emery Wilde." Her words thrill me, and I can't help but smile.

CHAPTER SIXTEEN: INGRID

Standing in front of the massive windows in our Chicago hotel suite, I gaze out over the city and watch the snowfall. "Emery, the snow has started again."

Emery wraps her arms around me from behind, pulling me close, "Yes, it has, and it's beautiful. These past three days with you have felt like a mystical dream, Ingrid."

Turning around, I pull her to me and hug her around the waist. "It's been beautiful, Emery—so romantic and loving. I think we've spent most of it in the bedroom or the tub," I say, then start laughing.

"We have indeed. Did we actually see any of Chicago?"

"Well, yes, just look out this window." Emery roars with laughter.

"Don't forget we have a view from the bed and the tub, so we *have* seen Chicago," Emery says, still laughing. She then grabs me and spins me around as we both laugh. "We've experienced every part of Chicago inside this magical Snow-Globe, Ingrid."

Laughing, I say, "Yes, we did, Emery," as I kiss her soft lips.

"Are you packed and ready for the train to take us to Denver?"

"Yes, ma'am, I am. What time does the train leave?"

"Two o'clock, so we should be on our way shortly."

"Okay, Ingrid. Give me a minute. I'll be right back." I smile at her, then turn back to the cityscape and continue watching the falling snow that has captivated Emery.

Feeling Emery's presence close by, I turn to her, and she smiles. "I have a gift for you, gorgeous." She steps closer and hands me a soft velvet pouch that feels heavy.

"What's in here, love?" I ask with a smile.

"This is the first gift of many, Ingrid," she says with a charming grin.

Playfully, I shake it to see if I can hear its contents. Emery laughs and says, "It's funny that you shook it."

Not understanding her comment, I slowly open the pouch and reach in gently. Emery holds the pouch as I pull out the gift. My eyes widen and begin to pool with tears. "Emery, my love, it's wonderful."

Shaking this lovely SnowGlobe, I gaze at her and see her love for me. Looking back at the globe, I wait for the dancing snowflakes to settle, and then I see the writing in the middle: *'Chicago.'*

"This is the most precious gift I've ever received, next to your love note." Shaking it again, I giggle as the flakes swirl and dance. "Our wonderful SnowGlobe. I don't want to leave this place, Emery."

"Whenever you want to daydream about the first time we made love, all you have to do is shake this globe. All our intimate moments from our time in Chicago will come flooding back to you."

Drawing Emery close, I place the globe on a side table and wrap my arms around her neck, pulling her tightly against me. "Thank you, Emery. I'll shake it every day for the rest of my life." She pulls me to her and holds me close. "I'm so thankful for you and your love."

Emery pulls away, puts her fingers through my hair, and then kisses me deeply and slowly, as if she's making love to me. I pull her close, threading my fingers through her thick hair and gently grip it with both hands.

Feeling her tongue swirling against mine sends intense waves through my sensual region causing me to shiver. I'm immediately on fire for her. Breaking our kiss, she looks at me and says, "I'm going to take you."

"Then take me, Emery. We only have fifteen minutes, so you better make it worth my while," I say with a grin.

Emery unzips my slacks and then slides her soft hands down the sides of my hips, catching my panties, pushing my slacks and panties down in one slow push. As she kneels on the floor in front me, removing my garments, I gaze at her with a grin. She glances up at me, and I says, "You are a wicked girl, Emery Wilde."

Remaining on her knees, she places her face against my feminine mound and begins smelling me. Pulling me open, I feel her warm tongue against my clit, giving my aching clit long, hard licks. "Oh, Emery. Honey, I have to sit." She grabs my ass, and looks up at me shaking her head.

"No, Ingrid. I'll hold you." Then she continues.

Suddenly, her fingers are deep inside me, pushing upward with slow, tender thrusts as she continues loving my clit. "Oh, Emery, that feels incredible."

Gripping strands of her lovely hair, I stand facing the falling snow as my lover takes me as she wishes. "Emery," is all I can whisper. She is licking my clit with her whole tongue, moving it slowly, then she flicks upward. All I can do is stand and let her hold me upright as we ride this together. We've found a tender rhythm to which we move in unison. "Yes, love," I whisper.

I continue watching the falling snow as my orgasm peaks. Gazing back into Emery's loving eyes, I nod and smile. She locks her hand against my ass to keep me steady as I begin to freefall. "Yes, Emery."

Looking up at me, she gives me two hard thrusts deep inside my core, and I feel myself letting go, "I'm coming, baby," I say breathlessly as I gaze at her loveliness. Closing my eyes, I feel myself growing weak as I release. I grip her hair and whisper, "I love you." Emery pulls me gently down to her, then wraps her strong arms around my weak body, holding me tight.

"Ingrid, my life is so vivid with you in it. I feel so alive with you." Smiling, I pull her close, wrapping my arms around her neck. We embrace savoring these last tender moments in our SnowGlobe. Pulling away, I look into her eyes, thread my fingers through her thick, sexy hair, and smile at her.

"Emery Wilde, you have no idea how incredibly happy you make me," I say with an emotional chuckle. I gaze at her pouty lips and kiss them tenderly. Pulling away, I look at her and add, "I love you, princess."

She looks at me and grins. "You taste incredible, Ingrid," she says as she touches my face, and then helps me back into my panties and slacks. "I love you, Ingrid. You make me so happy, and I don't mean just sexually."

"Emery, honey, I know that. But you do enjoy me sexually. Don't you?" I ask with a wink.

Continuing to help dress me, she giggles and says, "I'm like a cat in heat with you, Ingrid."

Laughing, I say, "Damn, Emery, that's quite a picture you painted for me." Standing up, I continue laughing. "We must get moving if we're going to catch that train."

"Well, if we miss it, we can just come back here and fuck all day and night."

"Damn you, Emery Wilde! Grab those bags and open that door; we have a train to catch. As we walk out the door, I glance over my shoulder and whisper, "You can fuck me on the train." Then I *meow* at her.

Walking to the elevator, we burst into laughter, our giggles echoing through the lobby. We leave the hotel, catch a taxi to the train station, and wait to board the train to Denver.

CHAPTER SEVENTEEN: EMERY

I ngrid and I stand on the train station concourse, waiting to board the Denver Zephyr. "Look at this train, Ingrid—so sleek and shiny; it's very impressive. From what I read, it was updated last year. We're going to enjoy the scenery through those large windows."

"Maybe this snow will travel along with us, love."

"Hopefully, we'll be encapsulated in another magical SnowGlobe in Denver," I whisper in her ear, inhaling her scent.

"Hmmm, that's a lovely thought, Emery."

Closing my eyes, I imagine Ingrid running into my arms at the airport. A smile spreads across my face as I gaze at her, reflecting on how our time together has flowed so seamlessly, filled with love and laughter. As I take her hand, she immediately intertwines her fingers with mine, a perfect fit.

After finding our private Pullman, we sit back on the plush cushioned seating. "I love this sofa; it's incredibly comfortable and very luxurious. By the way, when we left our hotel room, what did you say I could do to you on the train?" I ask Ingrid playfully.

Ingrid stands, then eases her voluptuous body down onto my lap as she straddles me. Grabbing her ass, I say, "You can whisper it in my ear so no one will hear."

Giggling, Ingrid wraps her arms around me as she gazes at my lips. Placing her wet tongue on my bottom lip, she lets it travel against my cheek all the way to my ear. "I said you can fuck me on the train." She whispers seductively, then *meows*.

Immediately my body has a profound response, rendering me halfway between climaxing and passing out. "Damn, woman! You have no idea what you do to me—every nerve ending feels like it's constricting with pain."

"Emery, baby, are you okay?" she asks with a chuckle.

"You're just too much at times, Ingrid," I say as I grab her hands. "I don't want to sound like a young, inexperienced lover, but at times, I feel overwhelmed by you."

"Emery," she whispers as she pulls me close against her. I feel that way with you too sometimes. At times, your immense passion for me is almost too intense, and I don't know if I can keep up," she says with a grin.

"Good, now I don't feel so foolish."

"Of course, you aren't foolish; you are a young woman in love." She looks into my eyes, and says, "Thankfully, I'm the woman who won your heart because I would have burned with jealousy if you had found someone else."

"Really?" I ask with a grin. "What if I had shown up at the airport with a woman?"

Ingrid pulls back and looks at me. Her expression turns serious as her green eyes blaze. Then she says in a cold tone, "I would have carved her heart out with a hunting knife and left it with the porter to dispose of."

"DAMN, Ingrid!" I begin to chuckle.

"Don't you ever ask me a question like that again, Emery," she says as she rises from my lap.

Pulling her back down, I hug her and say, "I'm sorry. I promise I'll never ask you something so asinine ever again. But damn, I did enjoy your answer." Ingrid still wears a serious expression, but it's starting to soften. Grinning at her, I see her coming back to me.

Ingrid threads her fingers through my hair, giving me a vehement look that makes her feelings unmistakably clear. "You are mine, Emery Wilde."

"Of course I am, Ingrid. I've been yours since I wrote that love poem years ago."

Gazing into my eyes, her expression softens. "I'm sorry, Emery," she says, huging me tenderly and kissing my hair. "I don't know why that drove me insane."

"Baby, It's okay. I rather enjoyed it," I say with a giggle. Ingrid begins to chuckle, then pulls away to look at me, and then we both burst into laughter.

"Emery, my burning desire for you made me completely irrational for a moment."

Still holding her, I grin and playfully add, *"Meow."*

Ingrid throws her head back and roars with laughter. "You're so naughty," she teases. Snuggling closer, she licks my bottom lip once more and then begins to purr.

Holding hands as the Zephyr glides swiftly along the tracks, Ingrid and I marvel at the snow-covered flatlands, and the gently rolling fields of Illinois. "This is amazing, Emery. God, how I'm enjoying this trip with you," she says, her voice warm.

"It's been incredible, Ingrid. I miss our suite in Chicago, but I know there's more magic for us to explore." Sitting up, I say, "Come here, baby. I want to hold you."

As she moves into my arms, Ingrid sighs. "You are so good

to me, Emery." Hugging her tighter, I watch the rural landscape through the large window as the vast fields gently pass by. I inhale Ingrid's familiar bergamot and vanilla scent. Closing my eyes briefly, I feel her warmth and love for me as I breathe her in.

Dusk is quickly approaching as we continue skirting across the snow-covered farmlands of Iowa. The small, dimly lit farmhouses spark my curiosity about the people inside, their lives, and who they are. "This truly is a winter wonderland, Ingrid."

"Yes, Emery. It is indeed."

I wonder how many people in these small farmhouses have seen your movies, Ingrid? Probably most of them, I bet."

"Emery, you're so sweet. That's a question I would enjoy knowing the answer to and would have never thought to ask. I live in a vacuum in Hollywood, and I'm tired of living that life—traveling like this is raw and real. It's exactly how I imagined it, but it's even better with you, love."

"I'd like to eat in the dining car tonight, Emery. I'll put my hair up, and we can sit away from everyone so I won't be noticed. Is that okay with you?"

"Of course. And I love your hair; it's so elegant. Are you hungry?"

"Yes, I am. We didn't have lunch, so let's find a table."

Seated at our table in the dining car, Ingrid and I savor a slice of pecan pie together after our meal. Glancing around, I see that no one is watching, so I offer Ingrid a bite of pie. She opens those gorgeous lips I've kissed countless times since we left Savannah.

Holding her gaze, I insert the fork filled with pecan to her mouth. She playfully rolls the bite off with her tongue, her eyes never leaving mine.

With the fork still in my hand, my head falls as I giggle.

"You're incredible, that was fucking hot," Ingrid chuckles at me.

"Emery, you shouldn't taunt me, lover." She giggles and then seductively asks, "May I have another bite?" Lifting the fork to her mouth, I offer her another bite, she swirls her tongue playfully around the pecans, and pulls them into her mouth. She then closes her eyes, moans, and she chews.

Dropping the fork, I grab my glass of water and begin to shake my head as I chuckle. "May I have another bite, lover?" she asks with a playful wink. Pushing the slice of pie toward her and handing her a fork. "You aren't going to feed your kitten?" she asks sweetly, then grins.

My feminine essence begins to pulse with pain as I watch her devour the pie with the same seductive playfulness. "You're loving this, Ingrid Mercer. Aren't you?"

Giving me a wink, she asks, "Do you mean I love watching you sit helplessly while I savor this pie, imagining it's you I'm feasting on?"

"Yes." I breathlessly whisper.

With one bite left, I pick up the gooey pecan filling with my fingers, place it in my mouth, slowly pull my fingers out, sucking the sweet residue off them, one finger at a time. Gazing at Ingrid's gorgeous lips, I chew the warm piece of pie with the same seductiveness.

Ingrid's mouth falls open, and she squirms in her chair. She leans into me and says, "Miss Wilde, you need to take me back to our private car now."

Not ready for our playful banter to end, I say, "Well, I don't know, ma'am, I barely know you." I say with a grin. "I mean, we've just met."

Ingrid snickers and says, "Listen here, I don't care if we've just met. I'm taking you back to my private compartment. You need to be taught a lesson, just like I told you in the taxi that night in Chicago."

We both begin to chuckle as Ingrid shakes her head and grins at me. Rising, I say, "Come on, baby. There is nothing I'd love more."

As we walk back to our private compartment, Ingrid takes my hand, and whispers, "You and I need to try out those plush cushions that you love so much."

"I intend on keeping you pinned down on those cushions for hours, Miss Mercer."

We both giggle in anticipation all the way back to our private compartment.

CHAPTER EIGHTEEN: INGRID

As we approach the Denver Union Station, Emery and I wait in our compartment to disembark the train. I smile and say, "Our snow is still with us, love."

"This beautiful snow is pure and fragile, like my love for you, Ingrid," she says, wrapping her arms around me and kissing my cheek sweetly.

"Emery, that's beautiful. Your love has always been so pure. You have no idea how many times I've revisited that night twelve years ago when you gave me your love poem."

Pulling me closer, she says, "That makes me so happy. I hated being only sixteen because I loved you so much and knew there was no way of having you." She says with a chuckle.

"I can still see your innocence and sincerity as you handed me that note," I say as Emery pulls me tight. "I waited until I went to bed to read it because I knew it was a love note and wanted to read it in solitude. It made me weep."

"It did?" she asks.

Nodding, I say, "Yes, I cried for a long time that night, not understanding why. But now I know why I wept."

"Why did you weep, Ingrid?"

"Because I, too, wished you weren't only sixteen, Emery."

"Oh, Ingrid. You were very much worth the wait."

"As were you, Emery."

The taxi driver loads our luggage into the trunk, and then Emery and I climb in the back seat, immediately huddling together. "Southern girls aren't used to this cold weather," Emery says with a chuckle.

"Where to, ladies?" asks the driver.

"The Cosmopolitan Hotel, please," I say.

"You smell incredible, Ingrid."

I whisper, "Thank you, love."

Emery pays the driver as we exit the taxi. The hotel bellhop greets us and takes our luggage, Waiting while Emery checks us into the hotel and secures our keys.

Entering our suite, I glance at Emery, who gives me a big smile. This is lovely, Ingrid."

After the bellhop leaves, Emery takes my hand, and we walk to the expansive windows facing the city. As we watch the falling snow against the city lights, I hug Emery, pulling her close. "Well, my love, it looks as though you got your wish. We're once again in another magical SnowGlobe."

"This trip just keeps getting better, Ingrid," she says with heightened excitement. As we remain embraced, watching the snow fall gracefully, we suddenly hear a knock on the door. Looking curiously at one another, Emery says, "I'll get it."

As Emery walks back from the door, she hands me an envelope. "He said this came a few hours ago."

Opening it, I see that it's a telegram. After I read it, my heart twists in painful knots. Silently walking to the bar, I pour myself a glass of bourbon and drink it.

"What's wrong, Ingrid?" Emery asks, her tone filled with concern.

Setting my empty glass down, I hand her the telegram. Seeing her face become fearful breaks my heart, so I turn away and pour myself another drink.

Emery lays the telegram on the bar beside me, walks to the vast window, folds her arms, and watches our innocent snowflakes fall tenderly. Reaching for the telegram, I read it once again, it reads:

WESTERN UNION TELEGRAM
To: Miss Ingrid Mercer
The Cosmopolitan Hotel
Denver, CO
URGENT: PLEASE CALL ME REGARDING
LEAD ROLE
IN A NEW MOVIE OFFER TIME-SENSITIVE.
Harold Bennett

Emery approaches me in silence, pours herself a bourbon, and quickly downs it. I take the bottle, put it back into the cabinet, then gently take her tender hand, and lead her to the couch.

Sitting on the couch opposite each other, our fingers interlaced, as they were that first night in Savannah, Emery gazes at me with vulnerable courage. "What are your thoughts on this, Ingrid?" she asks, her eyes searching mine.

Watching the snow falling just inches from our window, I shake my head and say, "I'm completely stunned. I don't know what to say, Emery."

Turning back to Emery, I see her gazing out the window, her eyes glistening. "What will you do?" she asks tenderly.

"Look at me, Emery. Please." Turning toward me, I see huge pools of tears in her eyes. Immediately, I move beside her and pull her close, But she remains stoic and doesn't return my embrace. Pulling back, I ask, "Do you remember how serious I was with you the night we first made love?"

Nodding, she says, "Of course, Ingrid."

"What did I say to you, Emery?" I ask, cupping her cheek with my hand.

"I remember what you said, but I want you to repeat it."

"Okay, I will. I said: *I want you to know I am committed to you.*"

"And I am still very much committed to you, Emery Wilde. There is nothing more important in my life, nor has there ever been, than you."

Emery forces a smile and nods at me. "You're never going to lose me, Emery. If you walked out that door right now, I'd hunt you down and bring you home to me, where you belong."

With tearful eyes, Emery says, "Ingrid, you have maintained that you are tired of your life in Hollywood. But, with this unbelievable offer, I couldn't blame you if you accepted. You're an amazing actress, and I'll never hold you back from the work you love."

"Oh, Emery," I say, threading my fingers through her hair. "My god, how I love your sexy hair." Feeling its softness between my fingers, I whisper, "I'm so in love with you, Emery."

Shaking her head, Emery whispers, "I know you are, Ingrid."

"Are you going to call him? Your agent."

"Yes. But you don't see me jumping over chairs to grab the phone, do you?"

She shakes her head and whispers, "No, I don't, but you have to be interested, Ingrid."

"Sure, I'm curious, Emery. But I've been making big plans for us throughout this trip. Plans that I haven't shared with you yet."

Looking at me curiously, she asks, "Like what, Ingrid?"

I stand up and look down at Emery. Smiling, I say, "Like buying us a big home on the beach near Savannah. I'm selling Mama's house. That house was her and Dad's dream home and my childhood home. But my dream is to have a home is with you, Emery.'"

"Let me ask you this, Emery: would you remain committed to me if I accepted this offer?"

Emery reaches for my hand, gently pulls me into her lap, and smiles, "I'll always remain faithfully yours, Ingrid."

With a huge smile, I hug Emery close. "Hearing you say that makes my life so much easier. I need to know you will remain by my side if I accept this offer."

"Of course I will, Ingrid. I'm in love with you. I've loved you forever, and waited so long for you. There's no way in hell I will let go of you."

"Oh, Emery. Baby, you have no idea how happy you've made me. I needed to know that your love is unconditional."

"Ingrid, how could you not know that?" she asks as she slowly pushes me onto the couch with her body. Gazing down at me, she says, "I'm simply scared of losing you. The telegram made me fearful that Hollywood would steal you and keep you locked away from me for another twelve years. My heart couldn't take that, Ingrid."

Pushing her pouty lips against mine, I kiss her tenderly, then pull away and gaze at them. "You have the sexiest lips I have ever known," I say.

"Nothing will ever keep me from you. There's no need for you to be fearful, love. It would be impossible for me to live without you, Emery." As we sit up, I look at her and say, "I'm going to call Harold back now. Okay?"

"Yes, please call. I will leave you alone to speak with him. I'm going to take a walk to clear my head. I don't want my presence to influence you in your decision."

"Well, okay, love. You won't be long, will you?"

Shaking her head as she puts on her navy peacoat she replies, "No, I won't stay long."

"Emery, I most likely won't have an answer after I speak with him. I will have to consider the offer and the part."

Gripping Emery's double-breasted coat, I pull it tight around her. "Stay warm, love."

Kissing her lips sweetly, she pulls me tightly. "Go call him; I'll see you soon." Emery kisses my cheek and then leaves.

Walking to the expansive window, I watch the snow and think about my future. As I get lost in my thoughts of Savannah and Emery, I catch a glimpse of Emery crossing the street and entering a coffee shop. Smiling, I turn and walk to the sofa.

Sitting on the sofa, I pick up the phone and dial Harold's office. "Good afternoon, this is Alice Sullivan speaking. How may I assist you today?"

"Hi Alice, this is Ingrid. Is Harold in?"

"Yes, he is Miss Mercer; let me connect you."

CHAPTER NINETEEN: EMERY

After entering *The Little Green Café*, I sit by the front window, my heart aching with pain. The glass of bourbon knocked the edge off, but the pain is still very much there.

"What will you have, dear?" asks the waitress.

"Coffee, please."

The waitress comes back quickly with a warm cup of coffee, and I begin sipping it to warm up. The snow continues to fall, just as it has been since before we reached Chicago.

I must support Ingrid if she accepts this role, but I don't want that. Gazing out the window, I remember how earnest and sincere her words were that night in Chicago: *"I want you to know that I am committed to you, and I always will be."*

She was indeed earnest. I've never seen her like that before. But I also realize that was before she received an offer to play the leading role in a movie that could rejuvenate her career again. That is what frightens me. It isn't the movie itself; she and I could manage being apart for one film. But what happens after that?

The waitress pours me another cup of coffee as I replay Ingrid's words from the couch on our first night in Savannah: *"Emery, all the leading parts go to women your age, honey."* Shaking my head, I realize this may be about her aging. I have no frame of reference for that at my age; I can't imagine how it might feel to have a lead role handed to me after I thought my career was over.

Sipping my coffee, I realize that I have to support this. Just as I asked Mama to accept my and her relationship for it wouldn't work, I now know I must embrace her decision. If I don't stand by her with love and support, I risk losing her, and rightfully so.

With that, I dash out of the coffee shop and head to a florist two blocks over. Walking inside, I'm greeted by a young and attractive woman about my age.

"Hello, I'm Nora. What may I help you with?" she asks, smiling at me.

"Nice to meet you, Nora, I need a dozen red roses and one white one, please."

"Well, sure, I can do that. Are you going to wait on them?"

Nodding with a smile, I say, "Yes, ma'am."

"Yes, ma'am," she repeats. You're Southern, aren't you?" she asks with a grin.

"I'm sure that's obvious," I say with a chuckle.

"You're beautiful, too. I love Southern girls," she says with a wink. *Oh hell*, I think as I turn around and busy myself with items in the shop.

"Where are you from?" She asks sweetly.

Approaching her, I reply, "Savannah."

"You are Southern!" She says with a chuckle." And I love your accent, by the way." Why do people always say this to Southern folks?

Shaking my head, I keep myself busy looking around.

Glancing at the top of a display, I see a silver star. I touch it, pick it up, gaze at it, and smile.

Walking back to Nora, I ask, "Will you please put this beside the white rose?"

"I sure will. What's your name?" she asks as she works with my order."

Standing close to her, I reply, "Emery."

"I like that name." She repeats it slowly, *"Emery,"* as she gazes at me." She puts the star next to the rose as I've asked her to, and says, "May I ask who these are for?"

Looking her dead in the eyes, I say, "The woman I've been in love with since I was sixteen years old."

Nora's mouth hangs open, and then she says, "Damn!" Picking the vase of flowers up, she sits them next to the cash register. "Well, she's a lucky woman, Emery."

"Thank you," I say with a smile. "I'm truly the lucky one."

After I pay for the flowers, I rush back into the fast-falling snow and start to laugh as I look at the star next to the white rose.

Entering the hotel suite, I rush to Ingrid, set the roses down, grab her in my arms and hold her tightly. "God, how I love you, woman. I love everything about you, Ingrid Mercer. And I always have."

"Emery, where have you been that's gotten you so excited?"

"Oh, just a coffee shop and then the florist. I'm sure you're used to getting roses. These, however, are the first ones from me, but they won't be the last."

Laughing, she looks at me and then the roses. "I love the white one, Emery."

"I'm glad. The white one is me, and the star is you."

"Emery, my love, these are beautiful. Thank you, darling."

"Come and sit with me, please," Ingrid asks as she takes my hand.

"Should I order champagne?" I ask with a grin.

"Well, yes, but give me just a minute. What has gotten you so over the moon and giddy?"

"Loving you, silly," I say as I kiss her cheek.

"We might need two bottles of champagne. I'm not used to seeing you this hyper and elated," she says, laughing.

"Well, tell me about the movie, baby," I ask, still hyped up.

Ingrid looks at me and says, "Well, I'm not going to lie to you; it's an amazing part, Emery. It's also one that I find somewhat humorous."

"What do you mean?" I ask curiously.

"Well, it's another *Film Noir* role. I'd play a former actress who has retreated to seclusion after a scandalous event, living in a decaying mansion haunted by her past." She chuckles, then continues, "The police find a dead body and discover the man is linked to her by a photograph they find in his home."

"That sounds interesting, Ingrid. I love all of your *Film Noir* movies—they're my favorites."

"I didn't know that, Emery," she says, looking at me with an odd gaze.

"Well, baby. I love all of your movies." I look at her. "You know, this is the first time you and I have really talked about them."

"You're right, it is," Emery."

"Well, I told you before that when I look at you, I don't see the big star that everyone else sees. I've always looked at you as a woman, Ingrid—a gorgeous woman who burns with fire and passion."

Ingrid touches my face and then kisses me sweetly. "Oh, Emery, my lovely woman, what did I ever do to deserve you?"

"You kept my love note close to your heart all these years."

Nodding, she whispers, "Yes, Emery. I did indeed keep your sweet love note."

Smiling at her, I ask, "When will they start filming?"

"Well, it's in pre-production now. They're still casting, working on set designs, hiring a crew, and acquiring permits. There's a lot that goes into it before they actually start shooting, and all of this could take months."

"Yes, I never thought about that. It's like how much work I must put into furniture before placing it on my showroom floor.

"That's a great analogy, Emery," she says with a smile.

"So, after these initial few months, how long will you be in Los Angeles for filming."

"Who says I'm going to Los Angeles?" Looking at her, I feel confused.

"Are they filming it on location?"

"No, most of it is on the sound stage as usual." Hell, now I really am confused. I search her face, but all I see is her beauty.

"I think you missed an important step, Emery," she says as she crawls onto my lap, straddling me as she did on the train.

"Damn, you can still render me helpless, Ingrid Mercer," I say as I gaze at her cleavage. Holding her ass in my hands, I pull her closer and whisper, "What step did I miss, Miss Mercer?"

"The part where I accept the film offer."

"Why wouldn't you accept it? I love you and want you to take this part."

"You do?" she asks, pulling away to read my face.

"Yes, Ingrid. I want you to be happy, baby."

"I am happy, Miss Wilde—happier than I've been in forever."

Holding her in my lap, our souls touch, and I feel her love. "Ingrid," I whisper. "Baby, you have to take this."

"I don't have to do a damn thing except love you for the rest of my life, Emery Wilde."

"But…"

Holding her finger to my mouth, she whispers, "Shhhhh." Then she removes her finger and adds, "Somewhere between when you left here an hour ago and returned, you must have hit your head against a rock."

I begin to laugh at her. "You're not taking this part?"

"Hell no. I'm not taking this part—I'm going to *LIVE IT!* Though, not in some decaying mansion with a dead man linked to my reason for seclusion," she says with a chuckle. "I'm living it with you, in a big ole house near Savannah, right on the beach, Miss Wilde. That way, you can seduce me on our private beach whenever you wish."

Ingrid's words hit me hard. I grab her and hold her close,crying uncontrollably, just like I did with Mama that day in my loft.

"Emery, I'm in love with you and I never want to know a day without you."

Pulling a tissue from the side table, Ingrid helps me wipe my eyes.

"Baby, it's okay," she says, holding me close. When you left here, I watched the falling snow and felt the emptiness of the room. As I stood there, I suddenly saw you walk into a coffee shop, and I knew then what I didn't want anymore."

Grabbing another tissue from the side table, I blot my eyes and look at Ingrid, "I don't mean to blubber like a baby."

Ingrid takes the tissue from me, holds it to my nose, and says, "Blow."

Bursting with laughter, I hug her. "What's so funny?" Ingrid asks.

"You and Mama are the only two women who have ever cleaned my nose."

Ingrid and I fall sideways onto the sofa,laughing uncontrollably. "Oh god, Emery, you make me laugh," she says. As our laughter continues, we hug each other with complete joy.

"I'm ordering that champagne NOW!" I declare loudly. As I rise from the sofa, still laughing, I lean down and capture her laughter with a kiss.

Picking up the phone to order the champagne, she says, "Oh Emery, don't forget to…"

"I know, Ingrid. I'll order some bread, too."

EPILOGUE

One year Later
January 1949
Tybee Island Beach Home

L illian and I sit in the garden room of the Coastal home, overlooking the Atlantic ocean. Emery and I built this beach dream home over the past year, and we couldn't be happier.

"Ingrid, your home here with Emery is breathtaking, but six thousand square feet?!"? Lillian says, as we both laugh together.

"Perhaps it's excessive, but I wanted to make Emery happy."

"Ingrid, that girl would be happy living with you in her loft," she says, as we continue our laughter and I shake my head in agreement.

"It's so wonderful laughing with you, Lillian. I'm glad we

have another back porch to sit on and solve problems." I say, gazing at my best friend.

"Ingrid, it's wonderful having you home again. A year ago, I wanted to strangle you and then bury your body, but now, I can't imagine Emery with anyone else. That girl loves you with a depth I've never seen in her, Ingrid."

"Lillian, Emery is my everything. I can't imagine my world without her. Why she chose me remains a mystery, but thank god she did."

We sit silently, watching Emery running on the beach with our Foxhound, Viola. Taking a sip of tea, I continue to watch them and ask Lillian, "Do you know that I call her my princess?"

Lillian's eyes glisten as she nods, "No, I didn't, but that's beautiful, Ingrid."

"Don't share that with anyone. You know Emery—she'd hate for others to know that I call her that."

"You're right about that," Lillian replies with a chuckle.

"The first time I called her 'princess' was at the Fox Theater in Atlanta last year during our Train excursion. It seems to fit her, and she loves it when I call her that."

Laughing, Lillian says, "I can't imagine anyone else ever trying to call her that. She's not a frilly girl like Anne, so I find it very amusing. However, you've touched a part of Emery's heart that I've never seen before, Ingrid. Thank you."

"Honey, you don't have to thank me. Our love is something that I didn't see coming. I wasn't even aware that she had loved me like this for so long. Emery completely swept me off my feet the moment I arrived that evening in Savannah. It was hard at first, given her age and the fact she's your daughter, Lillian. But, I couldn't walk away from her, nor did I want to. I would have been a fool."

Lillian picks up a scrip" on the side table and asks, "What's this, Ingrid?" as she examines it.

Sipping my tea, I reply, "A script for *The Glass Menagerie.*"

"By Tennessee Williams?" Lillian asks in a surprised tone.

"Yes. My agent sent it to me a week ago. They are revising the play and have asked me to portray the faded southern belle, Amanda Wingfield."

"Ingrid, that's absolutely wonderful, but honey, you are far from fading."

"That's kind of you to say, Lillian."

"What does Emery think about this?"

Grinning at Lillian, I say, "It was her idea. Last fall, when she and I were in New York, we went to a few Broadway plays. After one of them, we went to dinner. Sitting across from me, her eyes sparkled, and she said, "Ingrid, you would be amazing on that stage, baby."

"You would be Ingrid," Lillian adds.

"After she and I quibbled about it, she eventually won, as usual. Emery has helped me see that I am still a vibrant woman and would enjoy the theater." Glancing at the script, I add, "Harold, my agent, sent this last week. It looks like I'll be part of the cast in the revival of *The Glass Menagerie* for six months starting in September."

"Will Emery go with you?"

"She will stay with me on and off. The play will run for six months. I hate being away from her, but we will make it work. She is so good for me, Lillian, and she's even more excited about this than I am." I smile at Lillian as I speak.

"Honey, Emery has always been very intuitive and sensitive. Perhaps she understands that you shouldn't completely step away from the limelight that shines so brightly on you, Ingrid."

Shaking my head, I say, "You and Emery love me more than anyone on this earth, Lillian. I am truly a fortunate woman to have you both love me so much."

Lillian touches my hand and says, "We do, Ingrid. You're an amazing woman."

Emery enters the sunroom with Viola, kisses me, and then settles onto the loveseat. "Come on, girl," she says to Viola, who immediately jumps onto the sofa and lies beside her.

Lillian bursts with laughter. "Mama, what's so funny?" asks Emery.

"That dog on the couch," she says, as she continues laughing. I join her because I'm very aware of why she is laughing.

"Did I miss something?" Emery asks, looking at us both. Lillian and I continue laughing. Emery stands up and says, "Y'all keep laughing; I'll be right back. I'm going to get me some iced tea."

"Yes, Lillian, I know you find it quite amusing that I allow that hound in this house and on the furniture." We both burst again, almost uncontrollably.

"And I am very aware of who runs this household," Lillian says.

"You got that right, honey. I know my place."

Lillian continues chuckling as Emery walks back into the sunroom. "What are you two hens laughing at? It's normal for the two of you, but somehow, I feel like I am part of this joke."

"Emery, honey. You are, but in a good way," Lillian tells her.

"Well, okay then." She chuckles as she shakes her head.

"Oh, Mama. When I walked Daddy to his car, he asked me to let you know that he wouldn't be home until later."

"Okay, honey. Thank you."

"Who wants some wine?" Emery asks.

"I would love some, honey. Do you have some chardonnay?" Lillian asks.

"Of course, Mama. I'll be right back."

Lillian and I glance at one another, clink our tea glasses together, and laugh again. Just like the old days."

Emery and I hold hands as we walk the beach with Viola, our fingers interlocking sweetly and effortlessly. "I love you, Emery," I softly say as I lean against her shoulder feeling her warmth. Walking silently, we listen to the sound of the waves and we make it back to our coastal home.

Dusk settles as Emery and I retreat to the sunroom for the evening. I open a few windows in the garden room and I sit beside Emery on the couch. "Today was amazing with Lillian and Ted over, Emery. "

"Yes, it was, Ingrid," she says, taking my hand. "How do you feel about the script, baby?"

"I like the part, Emery. Amanda Wingfield is a complex figure—both charming and overbearing, not to mention middle aged," I say with a chuckle.

"Ingrid, you may feel middle-aged, but to me, you're still very much that same woman I've craved since my teenage years. The woman who burns with fire. The one whose flame keeps me warm at night and renders me almost helpless during lovemaking."

"Emery, have you always talked to women like this? Damn, honey. Your charm and compliments never get old, baby."

"No." She says quickly.

"No, what?" I ask, gazing at her.

"You're the only woman I've known whose soul and spirit burn so brightly, Ingrid. So, no, I haven't talked to other women like this."

Grinning at her, I rise and settle onto her lap, like she

loves for me to do. Emery immediately grabs my ass, as always, and looks at my cleavage and then my lips."

Holding me close, we listen to the waves breaking against the shore. "Ingrid, I am so incredibly happy." She pulls away to look at me and adds, "You, this home on our beach where I first touched you intimately—it's almost overwhelming at times. I couldn't be happier."

"Emery," I say as I pull her to my chest. "I'm home, finally, and I don't mean just Savannah. I have finally found my home. You are my home, Emery, and I've never been happier."

"I can't believe how much life has changed for us over the past year, Ingrid. Do you feel that too?"

Rising, I sit next to her and look out at the water, nodding. "Yes, it has, Emery. Selling my Hollywood home on Mulholland Drive wasn't hard, but letting go of Mama's house, where I spent my childhood, was somewhat difficult. But look at where we are now, princess."

"Well, you said in Denver that you were going to buy us a *'Big Ole House'* on the beach," Emery says with a chuckle.

Smiling at her, I take her hand and softly say, "Yes, I did. I knew exactly what I wanted at that moment and what I didn't want any longer, Emery."

"Now, a year later, I am so happy. Sometimes, I can't believe I share a beautiful home on the beach near Savannah with the same passionate young woman who gave me a love poem so many years ago."

"And now I share this beautiful home and life with the woman I love more than anything. The same woman who kept my tender love note safe, watched over it all these years, and then came home to *"Find Me."*

THANK YOU

Thank you for reading Escorting Miss Mercer. I hope you enjoyed it.

I'd love it if you could take a minute to leave a review on Amazon and let me know what you thought.

Thanks,
Aven

ALSO BY AVEN BLAIR

Claire's Young Flame

Julian's Lady Luck

Evan's Entanglement

My Sapphires only Dance for Her

Driving Miss Kennedy

Sailing Miss Clarkson

Flying Miss Lomax

ABOUT THE AUTHOR

 Aven is a passionate Sapphic romance author living in a charming Southern U.S. town with her wife and their two mischievous Chihuahuas. She crafts compelling narratives about strong Southern women navigating love and life, often set in historical Southern America. Her stories feature steamy age-gap romances, rich with warmth, humor, and depth, captivating readers with unforgettable tales of unwavering dedication.